The Cat tree and other stories

Martyn K Jones

All illustrations are by the author

Cover art by the author

Typeface: Times New Roman
Spell checker Oxford English Dictionary

Stobor Publishing

ISBN: 9781777040109

Contents

This collection is dedicated to those who can believe.

Especial thanks to my wife, Angela for having faith in me and also to Dr Kevin Hillman of Leg-Iron books for giving this sucker an even break.

Authors foreword:

As a schoolboy in the 1970's, I fell in love with the English language, a constantly evolving mongrel tongue, by turn capable of expressing the greatest grace and felicity, or of dripping poison more dangerously than a rabid pit viper. From age fifteen I've worked at improving what my late mother called my 'turn of phrase' into a style and voice of my own.

My mother tongue is the playground of poets, a veritable theme park for even the half-educated and a tool of communication by turns more varied and subtle than any other.

Since leaving school in 1974 my work has sporadically appeared in publications as varied as motorcycle and trade magazines, more latterly finding a small market in the supernatural / horror genre with my quirkier brand of comic horror story, like 'Moonlit Shadow', 'A Coelacanth in the bathroom' and 'Good here, innit?', all of which are included within this small volume.

The enclosed tales are the collected children of my occasionally troubled existence, each an attempt to make sense or even fun of, some facet of human nature, sometimes my own. Although which aspects I will leave to the individual reader's own good judgement.

So, please my good reader, take your dogmas off the leash for a romp around the fields with these, the offspring of my imagination. For this is what these stories are, my shared playground with the world. The light and shadow. Delve, skim, enjoy. Happy reading.

Martyn K Jones
21st November 2019
Victoria BC Canada

The Cat Tree

First written in 1983, this series of tales comes from a deeply troubled point in my personal life. Like my lead character Michael I had hit a personal low point. It was around this time I was 'adopted' by a mother cat and two kittens who were subsequently lost in similar fashion to the those outlined.

"Michael, good to see you, please sit." Paul checked Michaels psychiatric report, good to see him looking so much better. He'd responded to treatment and was ready to be discharged into a more homely environment, a place where he could regain his weight and strength.

Michael nodded absently and entered the tiny office, overcrowded with two mismatched castoff chairs, a desk and a single filing cabinet, all of which had seen long service. He was a tall, skinny man in his late thirties with lined, saggy features overlaid on a once-handsome face.

"Okay, first the good news. You can go home next week." Paul's artificial cheerfulness irritated Michael. Then his therapists 'professional' voice dropped a note; Michael almost winced. "But unfortunately, your wife refused. Well, you know the rest." Paul brightened again. "So we contacted other members of your family who suggested I talk to Mrs Harby. Your Aunt Elizabeth?" Aunt Liz?

A shaky memory of a large mid Victorian house drifted into Michaels mind, all oppressive heavy oaken doorways and cream walls. Right. Michael nodded dumbly, medication lying on him like a heavy fog, making coherent thought difficult.

"Who said she would give you a place to live while you got yourself sorted." Paul reached forward and patted Michael's unresponsive shoulder. "Better than a halfway house eh?" Again, the quick professional smile. "No lonely bedsit for you."

His psychiatric care worker must genuinely feel that he was doing him a favour, Michael thought miserably.

Paul glanced at the report again. Wondering how a rising star in the corporate firmament had fallen so far so quickly. Where had this man's wonderful life gone? The money, house, cars; and of course his beautiful wife. All washed away on a glut of alcohol. To Paul it just reinforced the futility of materialism.

Michael did not understand where his drink problem had started, only vaguely recalling some of the past few months.

The clinic with its shadow shuffling long stay patients a grey, drug fogged nightmare, its background susurrus of encouraging voices from nursing staff coupled with the constant sour mouthed craving for another drink. Now they were sending him back out into the world with nothing to hide behind. It felt scary, an awful prospect.

"Morning Michael. Wake up." The slightly plump silver haired figure of his Aunt Liz placed an unsteadily tinkling porcelain teacup on the dark oak bedside table. She smiled gently as he groaned his way into wakefulness. "Come on. Teas here. Drink it before it gets cold."

Michael sat up in bed, muttering sleep slurred thanks to his elderly Aunt. He shook his head as if that would clear the sleep away and pushed prematurely grey hair out of his eyes. He blinked. "What time is it?"

"Seven. Time you were getting up." What was going on? Since his discharge from the clinic she normally left him alone until at least eight. "Okay Auntie, what is it?" He sat up wearing old fashioned pyjamas and sipped at the hot, sweet tea. "Come into the kitchen and see." She was obviously excited about something; almost bobbing on her toes.

Half an hour later in the normally spotless pine and terracotta kitchen, a small group of chaotic creatures reigned supreme. Sitting proudly on the old-fashioned deal draining board was a purring tiger tabby cat. In the middle of the floor, three unruly, unhousetrained kittens craned their necks, fighting, tumbling and bumbling over each other in an attempt to gain their mothers attention and milk. "Aren't they gorgeous." Aunt Liz crooned delightedly.

Michael carefully skirted around the black, white and ginger comedy of kittens and placed his cup and saucer carefully in the sink. He jumped back.

The mother cat sat down again, wondering what had made the male human start like that. She had carried her children one by complaining one to this warm, safe smelling place for the humans to feed. Surely if she purred and showed affection they would give her food? Was that not the bargain?

"Quite." Pets had never figured much in Michael's upbringing.

"It seems we've been adopted." Aunt Liz smiled.

"Rather, yes." Michael reached out tentatively to the Mother cat, which allowed him to scratch her gently behind the ears. Her purring increased in volume and she ecstatically rubbed her head and neck against his nervous hand. Michael got over his initial surprise to enjoy this curiously pleasant act, all at once surprised and amused by the sheer lack of shyness.

"So what are we going to call them?" Aunt Liz picked up a panicking little ginger tom, which promptly sprayed her vinyl apron. "How about Puddles?" Michael chuckled, eyeing the droplets on her apron and the kitchen floor. Aunt Liz arched an eyebrow and pursed her lips in disapproval. "No, Marmaduke, I think." She kissed the complaining little fellow smartly on the nose and gently placed him on the floor. Stunned by the sudden change in altitude, the newly christened Marmaduke sat down heavily on the sun-warmed patch of red tiled floor. He looked up wide-eyed at a chuckling Michael and a smiling Aunt Liz, craning his neck until he fell over backwards. The two humans laughed out loud at the feline pratfall, the sudden noise startling the other two kittens who promptly pounced on their brood brother.

Marmaduke's mother gave what seemed to be a reproving glance at him for failing to retain feline dignity, then returned her attention to the pleasing sensation of being scratched under the chin by the strange, chemical smelling male. She watched each one of her children being picked up and kissed in turn by the elderly, Lavender scented female. Sounds that only meant something to humans passed between the male and female human as each kitten was picked up for inspection.

The ritual was of mild but waning interest; her place was elsewhere where the human who ruled did not welcome new children. Before, each precious litter had been taken from her too soon, much too soon. This house would be good, where her new brood would be safe and welcome. These humans smelled kind, as did the other presences. She stopped rubbing against Michael's hand and nodded greeting at the figures only she could see.

Slipping quietly as she had come, out through the open kitchen window she departed for home. Her three children did not notice as they busily gorged themselves on the delicious cool milk laid before them in one of Aunt Liz's best saucers.

"Hey! She's gone!" Michael suddenly noticed the Mother Cats departure.

"Oh, don't fuss so Michael, she'll be back. She wouldn't leave her kittens just like that." As always, Aunt Liz was unflustered.

The mother cat never returned. Less than half an hour later she lay dead in the gutter of a nearby main road, her small life halted by a speeding red hatchback, the driver too busy gossiping on her mobile phone to even notice the creature her car sent to oblivion. By the end of the second day, subsequent traffic and the ministrations of Crows and Magpies had reduced the mother cat's remains to scraps of dusty fur in the gutter, until the next heavy rainfall washed it away with all the other detritus.

Despite the loss of their Mother, the three kittens thrived in Michael's company. Michael seemed to spend a great deal of his free time playing with Marmaduke, Sukie and Roly as they romped through the large, semi organised Victorian garden. During the late spring and early summer, they chased anything that moved, birds, bees, butterflies and the occasional overconfident squirrel when the troubles began.

"Michael! Come and look at Sukie!" Aunt Liz's voice carried an unnatural edge of concern. Michael stiffly got to his feet from his accustomed resting place under the old Sweet Chestnut tree. Sukie, the smallest of the three kittens was having trouble, her hindquarters stiff and ungainly, normally upright tail drooping and immobile. "Hello little one." Sukie mewled a complaint as she was scooped up but did not struggle. "Better take you to the vet." Michael was hoping it was not too serious, but his voice carried doubt. "She feels very light – has she been eating okay?" He could still cradle her fragile feeling black and white body in one hand, that wasn't right. Aunt Liz furrowed her brow in concern. "Do you need any money?"

"No thanks, my part time job pays enough. I can afford the vets fees." At the moment, money was the least of his worries.

That afternoon he took Sukie tucked in Aunt Liz's old wicker shopping basket to the vets' surgery. Michael sniffed at the warm afternoon air, heady with the scent of unoccupied gardens and no traffic. He could really appreciate the summer blossoms now that taste and smell were no longer dulled by nicotine or alcohol.

Once on the green vinyl bench in the vets consulting room, Sukie feebly protested while the vet's cool professional hands prodded and probed. She stirred slightly as he took a blood sample, but not when he gave her an injection of antibiotics. "That should help until the results come through in about five days. I'll have definite news by then." The vet told him.

Five days passed and the news was not good. "Bad news my little one." Michael cupped the ailing kitten in the palms of his hands and wept as only men cry, silently and from the heart; tears splashing like summer rain from his cheeks and chin. This grief had a vicious life of its own, clawing at his chest whilst the ground seemed to have fallen from under his feet.

Sukie was given quietus at the vets later that day. Michael trudged home with a funereal gait to bury her lifeless form. He dug a deep hole near the base of the old Sweet Chestnut tree, the other two kittens watching cautiously as he laid Sukie to rest down amongst its roots. It just seemed like the natural thing to do.

A week later, disaster struck again. A neighbours Alsatian got into the garden, gleefully bounding after Roly and Marmaduke. An enraged Aunt Liz finally beat him off with a broom, but it was too late for Roly. His broken little body lay accusingly on the garden path. Marmaduke had to be coaxed down from the old Sweet Chestnut, ginger hair fluffed out in fright.

Michael was devastated. He buried Roly down among the tangled roots alongside Sukie and sat inconsolably with little Marmaduke in the kitchen all night. In the morning, Aunt Liz found a bottle of cheap vodka on the table in front of Michael's dozing form. Marmaduke blinked lazily up at her from his position on the kitchen table, purring loudly. Reaching round him, she examined the unopened bottle. So, he was getting better! Stroking Marmaduke's sleek ginger coat she asked thoughtfully. "Did you have anything to do with this?"

In late August they lost Marmaduke, finding his pathetically broken little body outside in the gutter; snuffed by another careless speeding car driver. This time Michael was too choked by grief to speak. After three silent days, Aunt Liz telephoned the clinic. "I'll be over next Friday." Paul agreed.

That Friday Michael withdrew to the top of the garden, book in hand. For a while, he stood looking blankly at the base of the old Sweet Chestnut. After a long pause he sat, back resting against the tree trunk, eventually dozing off in the late summer heat. As he slept, he dreamed of the three kittens still romping around the garden, their happier spirits somehow still here, helping give him the mental strength to overcome his weaknesses and grief. Was that a cat meowing? His eyes snapped open. For an alarmed second as Michael awoke, he could have sworn that the tree at his back was purring! Instead, he found himself looking up at Paul's professional smile.

"Michael. Good to see you. I take it you're feeling better?" As the care worker extended his hand, helping Michael up he paused. There was something different, more self-assured about his erstwhile patient today.

Michael looked blank briefly before giving Paul a curiously Zen-like smile. "Do you know what?" He replied. "I really do believe I am."

Polish Ted

Originally penned in 1987, this is a story based on several anecdotes as related by an old school friend who joined the UK Police in the late 1970's. While the stories of those I call 'the forgotten people' are very rarely found in the regular news media, unless it is a very slow news week, many die alone and unnoticed after long and very vital lives and who is to say that some of that vitality might not live on?

"Gi's it you old sod!" Sean lunged at the old guy in the tweed cap and jacket, intending to push him over for a laugh. Maybe nick his pension money; these old geezers loved carrying cash didn't they? Dead easy pickings, and Sean had got a thirst on for some readies, just to pay for a pint or two.

There was a moment of unexpected sudden movement, and cold grey paving stones cracked Sean's cheekbones, Burberry check baseball cap rolling into the dry, leaf clogged gutter.

"Get lost." Came the contemptuous, heavy middle European accented answer from the old man, who paused over him meaningfully before striding vigorously away down the narrow red brick terraced English street.

Sean found himself face down on the pavement, head aching, muzzily wondering how he had missed as everything faded to blankness.

"Oh look." Millicent stood in her old fashioned pearls and twin-set by the window, hearing aid turned down to tune out the background noise of Rebecca's hoovering. "It's Ted up and around again. That's nice." Regular as clockwork he as he ever was; ten o'clock every day. She'd missed seeing him stride up the street these past twelve months. Nice to see him back. Millicent let the ancient net curtain fall back into place and turned to smile gently at her home help.

Rebecca half ignored Millicent's comment and barely glanced out of the bay window at the old man walking purposefully up the terraced street. These old people lived in a world of their own; but still she asked, just for the sake of appearances. "Who's Ted?"

Millicent brushed a stray lock of permed silver hair back into place and tried to hold on to her smile. Rebecca was a nice girl really but bit of a milch cow. No real spark, no spirit, nothing exciting about her. Not the slightest urge to dress well either. Well, if she had any of those qualities she wouldn't be a bargain basement home help would she?

"Quite a man in his day." Millicent felt a warm thought bubble into her ninety-eight year old breast.

"Really." Was Rebecca's disinterested reply. Oh to have a day of the youth this bottle blonde woman was wasting, thought Millicent.

"One of the first commandos. If you believe the gossip down at the local Legion." Millicent tantalised. Still Rebecca carried on hoovering the faded floral carpet in that almost insulting manner of hers, as though she was only working under duress.

"Oh." It was clear the silly girl had no idea.

"Special Operations too, although you'd never think it to talk to him."

"What? SAS?" More of a contemptuous grunt than real interest.

"Oh no, before them dear."

"What was he, a spy or something?" Why was Rebecca being so sarcastic?

"No dear, he came over here in nineteen forty after Poland was invaded by the Nazi's. Joined the Army like a lot of his friends and carried on the fight. Won all sorts of medals. You'd think he'd walk lopsided on Remembrance Day." Millicent giggled for the first time since Rebecca had known her.

Rebecca looked at her sideways, lip curled in scarcely veiled disgust. Surely the old dear wasn't thinking about sex? At her age! Disgusting old woman.

Millicent caught the look but did not acknowledge it. These girls nowadays! You would have thought they'd invented sex the way they carried on. She could tell Rebecca a thing or two about the birds and bees. Not that the silly girl would believe her. Not that any of them would believe anything, even if it crept up and bit them on the backside. Just because you're old it didn't mean you'd never done anything with your life.

Millicent went back to looking out of the window. Ten minutes later, a scattering of red and blue light flashes announced an Ambulance pulling up at the top of the street. Wonder who that was for?

Sean awoke, looking into a bright light and instantly recoiled, right hand automatically trying to fend off whoever was doing this to him. "Good pupil reaction. Mild concussion." The voice came from a light blue clad blur. "All right young man." A firm friendly grip pushed his hand to one side and a fatherly dark skinned face swam into view. "What's your name?"

"Sean. Gerroff with that light willyer?"

"Okay Sean, you're in hospital. Now stop fidgeting." He was gently but firmly pushed back onto the tackiness of the plasticky bed.

Hospital! What! That old bastard had decked him. Him!

"What's your full name Sean?"

"Sean Wilson."

"Where do you live?"

"Who wants to know?" Sean grumbled sulkily.

"Hospital records. If we know who you are, we don't give you the wrong medicine. Right?" The Doctor blur admonished.

"Get lost!"

"If that's your attitude…" The Blurs voice sounded like he'd seen and heard all this before.

"Okay, alright. 32 Whetmore Street."

"Thank you." There was a pause as the figure wrote something down. "Headache?"

"What?"

"Have you got a headache?"

"Kind of, yeah."

"Mm-hm. Where?"

Sean pointed to his forehead, then felt at his left cheek which was covered by a dressing. It itched. As he did so he looked at his right arm properly for the first time. Who'd put this cast on him?

"Your right arm was fractured. Looks like you took quite a tumble." Was the Doctor Blurs blithe comment. "You also fractured your cheek when you fell. What happened?"

Sean was about to say "Some old fart done it." Then bit his tongue. What actually came out was "Dunno." As if he thought it would help he added. "Got jumped. From behind. I think there was three of 'em."

"Uh-huh." It was pretty plain the Doctor didn't believe a word. "Okay. Well you'll have to stay overnight for observation as you've been unconscious. Apart from your arm, there's nothing much wrong with you other than a few bumps and bruises." The Doctor stood up and stepped back. "There's a Policeman here if you want to talk to him." His lips twitched into a smile as he saw Sean's face jump in alarm. "Thought not. Okay Sean, I'll get rid of him." He handed his notes on to the Staff Nurse waiting behind him.

"Thanks." Sean lay back and breathed an ocean sized sigh of relief as the curtain was drawn around his little treatment bay. He didn't want the plods fishing around. That old fart was going to get what was coming to him. Petey and Jed would help; three of them should do it. Teach that old sod a lesson.

Detective Constable Charles nodded to the Doctor, and glanced through a gap in the curtain before leaving the bustling casualty department. Had someone finally bounced that nasty little scrote Sean Wilson? No convictions but the name kept surfacing in crime reports. No successful prosecutions and witness intimidation was often suspected but never proven. Still, the news that someone had taught him a short sharp lesson was not entirely unwelcome. DC Charles ran his hand through gel dressed dark brown hair and walked out, checking his cell phone for updates on his case list.

Be nice to have one little tearaway off the streets for a few weeks. Local crime might even drop. Trouble was; Sean would plan revenge with his pondlife mates when his arm healed. Charles knew he'd have to follow up and maybe have sharp words before it turned into a full fledged mini-gang war. If case load allowed. If he could keep Admin at bay with all their nagging emails and incessant demands for reports.

Just after eleven that morning, Rebecca shut Millicent's front door behind her, stepping into the tidy little street of English terraced houses. Her mobile shrilled. She listened and wavered a little as the news hit her. Her Sean in Hospital! Panic stirred her into unaccustomed action.

She bundled her heavy frame into her old Red Ford Fiesta, over revved the engine and crunched the gears before cutting sharply away from the kerb, causing another car to brake heavily. Horns sounded. She flashed an outraged middle finger, fleshy features creased in concern, not really thinking about the chaos she left in her wake.

Millicent heard the cacophony and sipped at the cup of weak tea she had managed to persuade the surly Rebecca to make her before she went. My goodness, it was getting noisy out there today. What was going on? She smiled at a familiar figure and gave it a little wave as it passed by her window.

The following day, the normally quiet Police station's front desk was in uproar. The Enquiries Officer, a white haired man in his late fifties, found himself facing the full molten fury of a mother in offspring protection mode. He forced himself to bite his lip while Rebecca screamed the place down. She had her eldest boy with her. A better case for late abortion he'd never seen, the man thought sardonically; he wasn't just thinking about Sean either.

"Are you listening to me?" Rebecca screeched, face distorted and red with rage.

"Yes madam. If you want to make a complaint…"

"I don't want to fill in your sodding forms – someone tried to kill my Sean!"

Pity they didn't succeed, thought the Enquiries Officer, carefully keeping his face open. He could feel the burn of the internal CCTV camera on his back, watching, forever waiting for him to make a slip that could lead to a disciplinary notice. All he could do was sit down and wait for her to run out of steam or storm out of the door. Right now either would do. She paused in mid flow, coughing. "Okay." The Enquiries Officer took out his pen and an Incident Form. "Tell me what happened and we'll put wheels in motion." He said with a practised professionalism he didn't feel.

"I don't want wheels in motion I want that old bastard arrested!"

"Right. Who did you say did this to your son?" The Enquiries Officer had chosen his moment expertly. Rebecca was stopped in mid tirade. Sean for once, had the good sense to remain silent.

"That old Polish twat from Highland Street!" She shouted. "Weren't you listening?"

"Do you know his name?"

"Course I don't know his fucking name! You stupid plod! Wouldn't be here otherwise would I!"

The Enquiries Officer put his pen down, folded his arms and looked Rebecca squarely in the eyes. "If you want to make a crime report or complaint, please do." He told her in stiff formal tones. "If not, stop wasting Police time." There. That told her. Get rid of the silly bloody woman.

Rebecca stormed out of the brick faced Police Station, pausing only to push Sean outside. "Bleeding coppers don't care about us!" She shouted as a parting shot. "Only care about filling in sodding forms!"

DC Charles walked in through the still swinging double doors a moment later. "Was that who I think it was?"

"Oh yes. Our 'Becca. Wanted some old Polish bloke arrested from what I could make out."

"Yeah, are they claiming some pensioner beat up little Sean?"

"Good luck to whoever it was. Any ideas?"

"No. All I know is an Ambulance crew picked up young Sean unconscious on the corner of Highland Street and West Avenue yesterday." DC Charles commented. "There are a couple of old Polish families in the area. I'll go and have a chat later on this afternoon. See if they know anything. Admin permitting."

"D'you think we've got a vigilante on our hands?"

"No. It looks like a one off. Maybe a mugging that went right."

"Don't you mean wrong?" The Enquiries Officer asked as he keyed the security door.

"No." Replied DC Charles, grinning at a random thought as he entered the main office. He'd been a street copper for a long time, and knew all about these inter family rows, they were the background noise he'd grown up with. A timely quiet word in the right ear was often the best way to deal with a situation and damn the bureaucracy. When you got time. When Admin wasn't trying to run you ragged. Walking past a stifled guffaw from the Enquiries Officer he headed back to his office to check in with his boss.

Sean was blushing furiously as only a nineteen year old being towed by his mother could. He wanted to sort it out himself, not get the sodding coppers involved. Rebecca bundled him into the front passenger seat of her car and slammed the door. The overstressed suspension bouncing as she literally jumped in. In her frustrated anger she stalled the engine twice before cutting sharply into the flow of traffic.

It was no good trying to talk to Mum when she had a strop on. Sean slouched back into his worn seat and sulked. He'd wait until everyone had forgotten this whole thing then he'd pay the old sod a visit, with some mates as backup of course.

Six weeks later over at Petey's place, Jed and Sean sat drinking Cans of Stella and trying to out – belch each other to a soundtrack of Rap music. At full volume it reverberated around the room, spilling out into the street. Petey and Jed cackled loudly at their successes and failures while Sean sat gloomily slumped in a bean bag at the back of the untidy room. He was still nursing his first drink while his mates were well into their third. They were supposedly celebrating Sean getting the all clear on his injuries. After a while he said. "I'm bored."

"What you wanna do?" Petey gurgled down the last of his lager.

"I wanna turn somebody over." Sean smirked with an evil leer. His skin still itched after the last dressing had been removed. A constant reminder him of payback to be made.

"Like who?" Jed was curious.

"Anyone. I want to have a bit of a laugh."

"All right." Petey stood up and farted loudly. They all laughed.

"Yeah." Jed stood up and tried to copy Petey. Secretly glad they didn't notice when his strained attempt failed to arrive. Sean was distracted and left his half finished can of beer, casually dropping his cigarette inside where it hissed out.

They picked up two baseball bats, stolen of course, bundling them inside the Hoodie Sean habitually wore. Petey slid an iron prybar up his right sleeve where it wouldn't show.

"Where we gonna go then?" Jed picked up his car keys.

"You drive. I'll tell you when."

"Okay."

That mid Wednesday afternoon the little market town's side streets were quiet for a change. Jed drove while Sean sat glowering out of the rear window at people in the street. Petey wound down the nearside front window, making insulting comments at them. "Get a proper sodding job!" He roared gleefully at a Traffic Warden, Jed revved the Volvo's old engine for effect. Bloody Traffic Vultures!

As they turned left into the Terraced row of West Avenue Sean saw exactly who he was looking for. "Here." Jed inexpertly swung the old Volvo into a parking place, two wheels inexpertly mounting the kerb. "Him." Sean pointed to the tweed clad figure striding towards them and got out of the car, slipping his hooded sweat shirt over his baseball cap just in case of witnesses or CCTV. Petey followed suit.

Jed reached under the drivers front seat to take out the second baseball bat and hid it behind his back. He walked up the middle of the street, circling around behind the tweed clad figure, closing the gap until he saw Sean's nod and swung at the old guy's head, hard.

Millicent saw Ted's familiar figure pass by her front bay window and waved as she always did. As usual he seemed not to see. It didn't matter anyway, he always knew she was here if he wanted to drop by.

What she saw next horrified her. Not ten paces from her front door, three young men wearing those scruffy hooded things went after Ted with vicious looking clubs in their hands. "Ted!" She shouted, her panicky voice pitifully weak. Oh no. Trying to control shaking hands, she picked up her telephone receiver and, arthritic fingers painfully slow, dialed the emergency number.

By the time the Police arrived it was all over. Sean, Jed and Petey lay on the pavement, massive head wounds oozing the last of their pointless lives onto long-broken paving stones. All three weapons lying bloodied on the ground close by. Ted was nowhere to be seen. An ambulance pulled up and the paramedics got out, emergency bags in hand. Millicent, obviously agitated, opened her door to the Policeman's polite knock. "Oh dear, officer." She quavered in considerable distress, tears in her rheumy blue grey eyes before a faint "Oh." Escaped her lips. "Oh dear." Her voice took on a deeper, calmer note as she saw Ted was not one of the bodies on the ground.

"Did you see anything madam?" DC Charles enquired solicitously. His colleague, a female Community Support Officer stood back and waited in case the old lady in the old fashioned dress needed a feminine touch.

"I saw those three young men.." Millicent's voice tailed off. A paramedic shook his head sadly before moving on to the next body. There was a crackle of radio messages.

"What were they doing?"

"They had those bats and they tried to attack Ted, er, Mr Pulaski."

DC Charles looked over at the Paramedics who had stopped trying to save life that was so obviously extinct. He drew a careful breath. "Where does Mister Pulaski live, Madam?"

"Number eighteen. Oh dear, is he in trouble officer?"

"I think we'd better talk to Mister Pulaski first." He said tersely.

At least the war was over. DC Charles sighed internally. Unfortunately he now had an OAP as a murder suspect. That wouldn't play well if the tabloids got hold of it. "Thank you for your help." He said carefully before walking the few steps down the street to number eighteen. As he passed the rows of rented properties that replaced a once tight knit little community, a sense of unease told him something was very wrong at the Pulaski house. Grimy windows and unwashed curtains choked with dead flies were all he could see when he peered inside. Already a hard lump of suspicion was forming in his mind. Pressing the doorbell, he heard it ring. After a minute he tried again. No reply. No shuffling. No sound at all. Not TV or radio. The female Community Support Officer arrived behind him and they exchanged a look of mutual agreement.

DC Charles walked through the brick built side entry and pushed open a peeling, weathered rear gate, leaving the CSO to carry on ringing the front door bell. Beyond the gate the narrow garden was a mess. Although everything seemed to be in place the back yard was overgrown, choked with weeds and brambles. Postage stamp lawn tussocky and untended. The windows at the rear of the house almost opaque, looking like they had been unwashed for the better part of a year. He could hear the Community Support Officer knocking on the front door and calling Mr Pulaski's name repeatedly. Then he caught a whiff of a particular musty flat odour. Once smelt, never forgotten. Walking back round to the front door he beckoned her down the passage. She grimaced as the smell registered. Both of them knew exactly what it meant.

A key left underneath a flowerpot by the back door saved them the trouble of breaking in. DC Charles opened the kitchen door and sniffed gently. "Call the coroners office and the Police Surgeon." He said tersely as the full strength of the dry musty odour caught in his nostrils.

The tiny galley kitchen was clean and bare, downstairs front room white painted, almost starkly so, a threadbare rug covering dark stained pine floorboards and little furniture. A few framed pictures hung slightly askew on the walls. Several were black and white photographs of young men in uniforms grinning across the years. Two chairs and a sofa pushed back to the walls and curiously, no TV. In the narrow front hall, a scree of junk mail and final reminders cascaded down from the letter box to the bare wooden floor, littering it with sundry bureaucratic threats and gaudy free offers of never to be missed opportunities long since expired. He kicked it aside, scattering the pile. The front door stuck and shuddered as he shouldered it open for the paramedics. Walking gingerly up the narrow stairs he followed the smell to its source. Just before opening the door, he turned to the Community Support Officer. “You ready?”

She nodded, face taut. She'd seen this before. "I wonder how long?"

"That's one for the coroner." He answered, trepidation tying his stomach in knots. He pushed at the door which swung wide open with a muted squeak.

Theodorus ‘Ted’ Pulaski lay neatly on his dead fly scattered bed, a dried out, part mummified husk, scraps of maggot-ignored sinew clinging to a dirty shrink wrapped skeleton. He'd died wearing his tweed suit. Regimental tie still knotted neatly. Around him the bedding was stained with a long dried brownish tidemark and his many medals lay in an open case on the dust and fly-strewn dressing table. A neatly arranged silver plated gentlemen’s grooming kit lay next to a dusty beret bearing an unfamiliar regimental badge. A second well worn Harris Tweed suit and six ironed white shirts hung dustily on a rail in an open wardrobe. Two other pairs of highly polished black shoes lurked under the dust by the bedroom window. Otherwise the room was neat but bare, with plain white painted walls and fading plush curtains. Pulling on a plastic glove PC Charles saw what was illuminated by the rooms solitary light bulb. “I’ve seen worse.” He said to himself, seeing more flashing red and blue lights pulling up in the street outside. “Let them in. Not that they can do anything for him." The CSO gratefully retreated downstairs.

The Police surgeon arrived next, a neat little man in a pinstripe suit smelling vaguely of formaldehyde. After a brief examination he decided death must have been by natural causes some twelve months earlier. Subject to autopsy. The Police surgeon shook his head at an arriving Paramedic, who went back down to the Ambulance for a body bag. The body would be removed to the local hospitals mortuary for post mortem and no doubt enquiries begun to find any next of kin.

DC Charles watched the body being delicately placed in a black plastic body bag and shook his head gently. Mrs Jellicoe must have been mistaken. Not really surprising at her age and state of health. So who the hell had those kids really gone after? A brief round of door knocking unsurprisingly produced no answers. Mr Pulaski was one of the great forgotten, people who lived, then simply vanished because there was no one left who remembered them.

The following day Millicent was pleasantly surprised when her doorbell rang. On her doorstep was the man himself. "Oh Ted! You shouldn't have." She said, taking possession of the single red rose he'd brought with him. "Come in and have some tea." He was such an old romantic. "Nice to have a gentleman caller for a change." She giggled a little self consciously.

As the kettle boiled and Millicent fussed over the ritual of cups and saucers, they discussed the previous days events. "As for those boys Ted." Millicent chided. "You shouldn't have tricked them into hitting each other like that. That was wrong. Very wrong indeed."

"So? They try to kill me." Ted Pulaski laconically rumbled from his preferred place in the chintzy high backed armchair by Millicent's rarely watched Television.

"But that's different, Ted." Millicent's reproving voice echoed out of her neat bright little kitchen. "You're already dead."

Moonlit shadow

First written in November 2018 specifically for the Christmas Underdog anthology, 'Christmas lights and darks' this was my first ever attempt at writing a Christmas themed horror story. Just a little fun mix and match mythology. I would like to take this opportunity to reassure readers that no reindeer were harmed in the writing of this tale.

Tonight the moon is almost daylight bright and the world around the derelict old house is a vivid monochrome. Inside a room with two broken old chairs and a stinking mattress on the floor the stillness paints itself around graffiti-scarred broken plaster and lathing. The ceiling is partially collapsed with gaping holes leading up to a space so frozen that even the pigeons have left. A deep frost makes flaking brick and peeling wood glitter. Winter is here in all its crystal majesty.

Across the fields comes the sharp acid scream of a fox calling for its mate. Nocturnal rustlings from foraging badgers and rabbits in stark hedgerows. The spectre of a rare barn owl gliding across an eerie moonscape. All else is silent but for the night breeze gently rattling dried leaves in stark branches.

A heavy truck taking a shortcut down the secondary road outside rumbles its laden way to an all night destination. The forty tonne trailers grumbling setting up sympathetic vibrations in dessicated timber, fine dust drifting into still December night air, curling, shifting, following invisible lines around a shape, silent as smoke, less visible than whispers. Tenuous. Unformed.

Ah. Comes the word of consciousness. Softer than a sigh on the wind, colder than the night between worlds. Airborne dust follows lines in the air, highlighting the shape like stars around a nebula, a gravitational lens bending light so even the untrained eye can detect the hidden, the lost, the infinitesimal. The shape in the air moves through the dust like a living shadow, a bulky, hooded figure shrouded in brilliant motes.

The breath of awareness flickers into words at the very cusp of hearing.

I see. Must I?

There is consciousness here. Volition. The bitterness of self knowledge and reluctant acceptance, even a deep, long suffered anguish.

The figure raises barely visible mittened hands in front of a deeply hooded face, examining them as if for the first time, turning them back and around.

Yes. The duty.

That which must be done tonight and at no other time. The obligation. The necessity. This spectral whisper carries centuries of pain but asks the question of the moonlit air.

For how much longer?

The hooded head bows forward, hands dropping to the sides of a primitive belted tunic worn over old fashioned baggy breeches tucked into heavy night-black boots.

Was my sin so great? My insult to God so grievous that I must suffer forever? I was an Angel once, beloved of our creator. I brought light to his lesser cosmos so the humans he created could love him more completely.

The figure gradually coalesces in the moonlight, fading into view oh so slowly, taking on form and solidity.

Humans called me the bringer of light. *Why Lord, why must I still suffer for the love you withhold from me?*

As if in answer, a breath of midnight wind blows through a glassless window. The shape shakes rhythmically as though sobbing.

Please.

Begs the shape as it coalesces into a shadow-form.

No.

The tone is pain-wracked and plaintive.

From outside comes the vague noise of ghostly bells. A tinny rustling like millions of empty cans rolling downhill. The shadow groans softly. Eight distinct non-human voices, a chorus of soft grunts, urgently basso-profundo calling to the reluctant figure.

Come. We are here. It is time.

They do not question their eternal fate, but then they were never angelic, never aware. All these shadow-beasts know is the thrill of side-slipping across time and space, revelling in their headlong gallop through glittering starlit portals. The roller-coaster joy of tendon, sinew, bone and muscle singing together through their high speed Möbius trans-dimensional journey.

This is their life, but also his fate. Here is where his shame and agony lies.

An eternity ago he was not this lumbering human caricature but a vibrant harmonic figure, a messenger of God, joyous and exuberant, a dazzling light streaking across the firmament. Now he is confined, demoted to the mundane task of keeping a simple foolish belief alive in this backwater of creation. A figure of pity, not even scorn.

Then he breathes in the chill of the night, tasting the frigid air and a distinctly un-angelic cough breaks the silence as cold air snatches the back of his throat. At first it is the cough of an old man. A retching, tinny sound punctuating the shadow taking on a lighter shade of grey in the brilliant moonlight. The shadow form flickers as he coughs again, each hacking catch a new step towards reality. Now he gains substance and weight, ancient floorboards flexing slightly under heavy-soled riding boots, leather black as the darkest cellar with sinuous stamped patterns that shift and writhe as though they were sentient.

Now he sniffs deeply at the air again and his snort is of something deeper, more animal, like the grunting cough of a hunting Grizzly. This is life. The figure remembers this song and feels it like an ache in his bones, an opening of eyes.

Then, as if absent mindedly recalling a half forgotten task, and still only semi visible, the figure turns to the scabrous mattress lying on the floor. A small token is necessary. A promise must be kept. He bends over and reaches down into a hummock of mixed blankets and fleeces in the shadows, mitten passing through as if there was nothing there. There is a faint sound half way between a sigh and a cough from underneath the heavy layers of fabric.

Thank you.

The figure twists something around a mittened hand that for a moment gleams like a fish, then is gone.

I will keep it safe.

Whatever is under the blankets sags slightly and there is a sense of deeper stillness in the freezing room.

A year. That was the promise. Then eternal peace. The moonlit figure straightens up listening to the tinny rustling and grunting urgency only he can hear.

A few moments, please.

The unheard request seems to calm whatever is outside and the noises grow quiet. There is a little time for reflection before the duty begins. A respite.

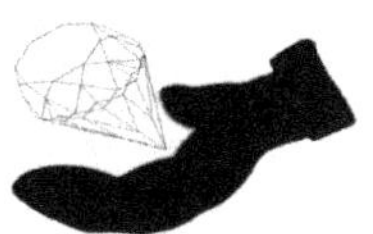

Three hundred and forty three days ago the figure had sat with the old man whose soul will fuel him for the next few hours between dimensions. An old man who was so used to his pain he rarely remembered it. An old man who knew he was dying. Clawed from within by his 'old enemy' as he had called it. Before the mask dropped and his agony leaked out.

That pain had reached out to the figure as he passed down a midnight street where Tommy Cawley, or 'old Tom' had been lying slumped against a urine stinking wall, empty bottle in hand, semi conscious and wishing for the night to claim him. Whether that was his real name or not no-one else cared. Tommy's old name was back in his past, in the wreckage of a former life. Before his fall from polite society, before the cancer had come to eat him alive. Until a tall, stout figure in a belted tunic stands over him and says gently. “Hello Christopher.”

“That's not my name.” 'Old Tom' slurs defiantly.

“Would you die with a lie in your mouth?”

“Get los' you fat bassar!” The old man drunkenly snarls from the gutter.

“Do you know who I am?”

“Don' fuggin care. Lemme be.” The recumbent figure tries to turn away, broken down trainers scrabbling pathetically at unforgiving concrete.

"You should care, because I have something very valuable to offer you." In the rain slick midnight street the hood slides back. All the old man can do is stare.

"You're..." The old man seems transfixed. Eyes wide and horrified.

"Yes." Says the figure. "We should talk. Let me buy you some tea."

Later, in the corner of a late night cafe the two sit like old friends. Voices low and conspiratorial. "I can't go back." Christopher says.

"I know."

"But I just want to see her again. Just one more time. Before I die. Am I dying?" Christopher Thomas Cawleyson is lucid for the first time in many years.

"Yes." There is no point dodging the issue.

"Are you here for me?"

"Yes."

"When? Am I..."

"Enough." The stout figure stops him with an upright hand. "Not yet. I can give you a year. No more."

"What if I say no?"

The figure takes a thoughtful sip of tea. "Then you die tonight. Back in the street where I found you."

"Is that a threat?"

"No." The figure seems amused. "This is an offer of life, not death. You can do a lot in a year." He purses his lips thoughtfully. "Lay ghosts. Mend fences. Turn corners. Or at least help those in trouble turn the right ones."

Christopher Thomas Cawleyson, Veteran of Iraq. Bankrupt, alcoholic, bad father, worse grandfather, stares at the chipped laminate tabletop. "I'm not a good man." He says eventually.

"I know."

"I don't know if I deserve this chance."

"You do. She does."

"Thank you." The old man leans forward a little. "Okay. What do I have to do?"

"Nothing much. Only what I ask you. Nothing you can't do."

"For a year? For redemption?"

"Yes."

"Not for me. For her." Christopher says, eyes fierce.

"Agreed." And they, very gravely, shake hands to seal their compact.

That was twelve days short of a year ago. Satan, fallen angel, now fully in mortal form, opens his glove to examine the spinning crystalline form that had once been the life force of an old man in pain. When he had first seen this soul it had been damaged, cracked and filthy. Not even worthy of discard in some forgotten corner of Hell. Now it gleams, truly worthy of cherishing.

"Thank you."

Satan pushes back his deep red fur lined hood to reveal an old man's face, smiling and white bearded. In the moonlit shadows the soul sparkles and shines.

"Now you and I have a job to do." Satan says. He looks out of the abandoned room to the top of the stairwell. The grunts and tinny noises grow louder, more restive.

"Patience. I'm coming." He smiles at the soul and tucks the glittering thing into a leather purse at his waist. Pausing only to pull up his fur trimmed hood against the night he walks down the creaking stairs and examines the scene before him, reaching out to stroke a muzzle, pat a neck affectionately.

"Hello. Have you missed me?" The eight voices grunt with joy at their masters arrival. Satan takes his place and removes the soul from his purse, plugging it into a socket on the sleighs dashboard. "Are we ready?" He checks the massive bags behind him and notes their bulk with satisfaction. The eight voices grunt, heavy leather traces decked with fine gold and silver ornament, straining and jingling.

"Very well." Satan picks up a small whip and cracks it with a satisfying snap! "Up Dasher! Up Prancer! Up Dancer and Vixen! Up Comet and Cupid! Up Donner and Blitzen!"

With this command, powered by a single glittering redeemed soul, Satan's sleigh rose into the brilliant midnight of Christmas Eve.

Just another day at the office

When that once in a lifetime employment opportunity knocks on your door, is there sometimes a little wisdom in not answering?

This is the origin piece for the Dafydd Llewellyn-Evans series of comic supernatural detective stories which includes 'A Coelacanth in the bathroom' and 'Bats!'.

At the dead, dark end of a rain damp alleyway, the naked Cyclops skidded to a halt and stared back at him from in front of a high grey concrete wall, gummy mouth wide open in horror as if he were the monster.

Dave halted and blinked back, chest heaving with exertion, fascinated by the single large central eye which seemed far too big for the sparsely lank-haired head. “All right you. You're under arrest.” Dave wheezed, wiping sweat from rounded Celtic features. Damn, but the bloody thing could run!

As a Police officer he was supposed to be relatively fit, but this thing had led him a right merry dance through Cardiff's early morning side streets and alleyways.

While he had it backed into a corner, the random thought sidled into his forebrain that this ginger haired homunculus was more what you'd expect from Pixar or Walt Disney. It was a caricature, a cartoonists idea of what a single eyed creature should look like.

Then, just as he adjusted his handcuffs to snap them on the cowering creature, he felt a twist in the air, blinked and the Cyclops was gone. Thin air. Not so much as a puff of theatrical smoke.

Not again. That was the second time this week. Dave sagged, canvas windcheater sticking to his skin through a sweat soaked dark blue t-shirt. Within his lightweight hiking trousers, his thighs ached. Despite decent trainers, his feet did too.

Why had he taken this daft job anyway? Ah. Yes. Right. Boredom with the usual routine trawling of lists, taking statements and weaselling pallid lies from the wicked and weak willed. That and the promotion that came with it. But if he'd really known what this job involved, he'd have walked out of the door and gone to get totally weasel-arse drunk for a week. Well he might just do that tonight anyway. If he managed to get home before midnight.

Chasing 'anomalies' had turned out to be nothing but a right bloody fools game that had him tear-arsing from town to town at some ungodly hour only to find nothing but unsubstantiated reports. This time was different, the Cyclops had been haunting the underpasses and parks around Cardiff for two whole months, making dogs howl and cats disappear. The local Police hadn't a clue and couldn't be bothered so the case file had ended up on his desk. What was it with Cyclops and cats?

He'd never find out because now the mini monster was gone. Like a Tiger Bay fog. British X-Files my arse. More like Laurel and Hardy than Mulder and Scully.

Leaning against the brick lined alleyways wall to catch his breath he recalled how he'd ended up in this mugs game. He'd been summoned one Thursday evening to a meeting. The door to the Chief Superintendent's office had been open and Chief Superintendent Mangan sat behind the desk, a dapper looking civilian seated in front of her. "This is Detective Constable Llewellyn-Evans." The uniformed Chief Superintendent announced to the civilian, who carried the air of one used to the effortless wielding of authority. A sort of Sir Humphrey Appleby on steroids, thought Dave. "Dafydd." The Chief Super said.

"Ma'am?" Oh no, she even pronounced his first name correctly. Dav-i-th with a hard th, not Daf-id in her usual offhand English manner. Dafydd's mind raced. What had he done wrong?

"We have a request from the Ministry of Justice, via Mister Williams here. A job for which we think you are the ideal candidate." Oh God, the Chief Super was referring to herself in the third person, this was bad, very bad. Dave struggled to keep his poker face firmly neutral.

"As you have already passed your Sergeants exam, the job automatically entails promotion to Detective Sergeant as a senior officer in a brand new task force." She continued, her mouth smiling like a shark. Her steely grey eyes however, said 'gotcha'. She was obviously happy to have ticked yet another box on her way to Assistant Chief Constable.

Oh my, what big teeth she has. Dave thought morosely. On the other hand, he reasoned, senior member of a new task force? The extra money would certainly come in useful. He brightened a little. Promotion with benefits would get him out of a few minor jams with the credit card companies and his landlord. "Thank you Ma'am." He said with genuine sincerity.

"Mister Williams will fill in the broad operational details. I have another appointment to keep." She got up from her chair and with a clump of heavy heeled shoes Chief Superintendent Hilary Mangan was gone. Which was odd. Surely this was an operational matter she'd have to sign off on?

Mister Williams on the other hand, if that was his real name, stank of influence, from the top of his well-groomed grey peppered haircut to the tips of his shiny and very expensive black shoes. Well-cut suit, Guards regiment tie, smug, subtle cat-that-got-the-canary smile. Right. Wouldn't hurt to keep on the right side of him. Although if you opened him up, you'd likely find 'Property of Whitehall' tattooed on every major organ, especially his brain.

Williams stood up, moved easily to the other side of the Chief Super's desk to lean back in her executive leather chair. "Detective Constable. Or may I call you Dafydd" He said, pronouncing Dave's name perfectly then gestured at the chair he had just vacated. "Or do you prefer Dave?"

"Dave will be fine sir." Dave replied cautiously.

When he sat down on the slightly warm fabric Dave got the feeling his every move was being silently critiqued. Mister Williams looked over steepled fingertips from the Chief Super's chair at Dave, who kept his face utterly expressionless.

"We at the Ministry of Justice have a job we'd like you to do." Mister Williams launched into his sales pitch. "As Hilary said, it comes with automatic promotion to Detective Sergeant and full private health insurance cover. Including dental. With BUPA I believe." There was something about Williams small smug smile that made Dave want to punch it, very, very badly. But if this Williams character was going to get him a Detective Sergeants pay or better with full benefits, he could restrain himself from almost anything.

"What is the job sir?" He'd asked.

"You are a careful and assiduous officer of the Police service, yet your superiors think, and I tend to agree, that you have special talents which should prove invaluable for this role." Said Williams in tones so oily you could have fried chips in it.

"Which talents are those?" Dave asked, trying to look like a tough seen-it-all Detective Constable and failing. He often had the mickey taken for not looking enough like a real copper, trying to cultivate a steely thousand mile stare, but only ending up looking like he had a bad squint.

"You have a unique instinct." Williams said. "One which would greatly benefit the new anomaly task force."

"Anomaly task force?"

"Yes. You have a demonstrated talent for observing the extraordinary and finding the mundane. Like that case forwarded to the CPA last month. The, ahem... werewolf?"

"But that was a man living in a dog kennel because his wife had kicked him out for snoring." Said Dave.

"The initial complaint was about a werewolf." Williams insisted. "Then there were the UFO reports, which you correctly identified as an inebriated children's entertainer who kept accidentally releasing foil helium balloons." He continued. "You, detective sergeant, have a talent for the truth. And the truth of these matters is very important. Because much Police service time is wasted chasing after these chimeras and hobgoblins. This situation must end and you are the man we feel who can end it. Three years in post will see you promoted to Inspector. Not to mention the other benefits of seniority in such a specialist discipline."

Leaning against the wall, hands on knees and breathing hard, Dave wondered if the implied benefits were that great, if what Williams had said was true, why hadn't there been a mile long queue outside the Chief Supers office? Why was this job only offered to him?

He'd found a partial answer three months later in the internal Police service newsletter. A niece of the Chief Superintendent had just passed her detectives exam and been put on the fast track. She was now following a trail of career stepping stones to high office. One of which was Dave's previous lowly post in the regional crime squad.

So that was why he'd been given this once in a lifetime opportunity. He'd been shunted sideways into what Justice must have thought was a non-job. Only to find that it wasn't, the monsters were real. There were such things as Vampires, Werewolves, Leprechauns and Cyclops. Not to mention those bloody pixies who had taken up residence in his chest of drawers. Yes, it was nice to have clean, neatly folded underwear, but he lived in horror of slipping into a pair of briefs to find one of the little so-and-so's haunting his gussets. A bad tempered pixie, as he had found to his cost, was a formidable thing. The thought of one in close proximity to his important little places gave him the shudders.

Dave wiped sweat from his face, blinking heavily as he got his breath back. Right. Anyway, that bloody Cyclops was now gone, at least that meant Cardiff's cat population could once more hunt other small furry creatures in peace. Job done. Home for tea and paperwork. Just another day at the office.

He shook his head in resigned dismay and walked back to his car, only to find a parking ticket tucked under his cars grubby windscreen wiper. Bloody hell fire.

Good here, innit?

A twisted little satire of mortality and the futility of corporeal affairs written in 2019, appearing in the 9th Underdog Anthology, Halloween edition.

Premise; Imagine finding a very smart coat in a second hand clothing store, donning it and finding your world inverted. Falling literally from a metaphorical frying pan into an unfamiliar fire.

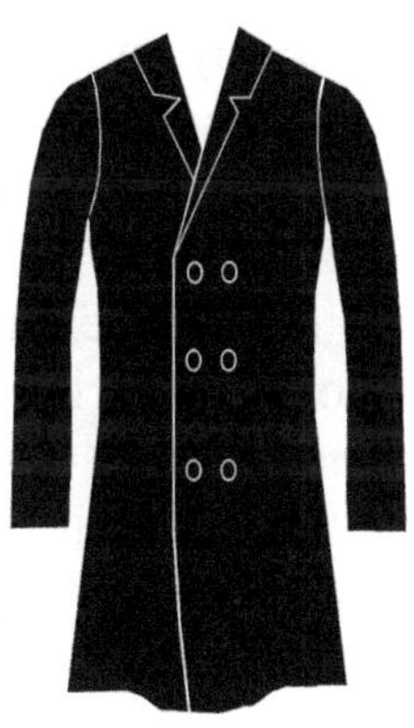

Wallace was disinterestedly rummaging through a rack in a dusty little charity shop when he recognised the quality. Good cloth. Nice schmutter. A fine cashmere if he was any judge. Cut a little on the old fashioned side, but early seventies eclecticism was making a comeback, so there was a ready market for those styles, especially at the top end.

This particular frock coat certainly looked like a real find. As new condition. Mmm. Interesting.

He checked the label on the inside breast pocket. Harry Mann. Saville Row. London. Cashmere Wool. Real gold thread in the label embroidery too. Very nice. A real find. Knee length, double breasted, lapels not too wide and an almost perfect black. Not your usual plain black-cat-in-a-coal-cellar charcoal but an all swallowing shade that looked like it snacked on black holes between meals.

Wallace stared for a moment and shook his head as if to clear it before natural avarice took over.

Bundling the obviously quality coat in with a bunch of lesser, but still fairly well cut men's coats he took them to the checkout desk. "Forty quid for the lot?" He asked in what he hoped was a winsome manner at the plain-looking mature student behind the counter. She paid his ingratiating manner little mind. She was too busy swiping left.

She glanced up briefly from her cell phone at the pile and gave him a shallow toothy smile in return. "Yeah. Forty. Lovely." And took the two slightly grubby twenties out of his hand before ringing them through an old fashioned till.

She didn't offer to wrap the coats. It was a charity store after all. But, she noted, it was a nice touch of his to leave the empty hangers. Most people just took them. Which so many didn't appreciate. Coat hangers didn't grow on trees.

Gingerly taking the proffered receipt, Wallace left the store, strolled around the corner and down to a side street to where he'd parked his old 1989 Daimler double Six. An underrated classic, but then Wallace had a nose for such gear. Pukka heritage kit was always worth good money to the right people. That was how he made quite a nice living. Find the good stuff cheap, spend a little tarting it up, then flog it to the highest bidder. All you really needed was the contacts. This particular coat should be worth at least two grand to the right punter. Maybe much, much more.

After folding his find carefully with fussy fine boned hands, he placed the coat in a large tissue-paper lined box he kept in the Daimler's boot, covering it with lower quality items. Closing the lid with a nice solid thud, he slid his spindly frame into the leather drivers seat and a little thrill ran down Wallace's spine as the smooth bass purr of the six litre V12 spun into life. The stereo, a cleverly disguised modern multimedia player, began playing an old 80's b-side 'moving in stereo', an old favourite. As he drove, Wallace happily thumped the steering wheel in time to its heavy, erotic, backbeat.

Avoiding main roads, he slipped steadily through a maze of narrow residential streets. Half an hour later pulling into a row of Victorian era railway arches, now closed off and used as shelter for a variety of semi-reputable businesses, including his. The automatic door opener swung a heavy garage door up and a welcoming inside light came on. The Daimler slid inside and the door closed behind the car with a satisfying clunk just as Wallace shut down the engine.

Swinging himself out of the drivers side door into the echoing space, he opened the boot and carefully checked his purchases once more, looking for flaws he might have missed.

Checking the gate he felt reassured by the outer door panels reinforced with heavy steel framing and solid brick. Which was good because only a determined thief would attempt entry. Not that any round here would try, given his carefully nurtured relationships with the local crime families, but there were enough desperate souls in this world and it paid not to put temptation in their path.

However, the local junkies weren't up yet. He was always out and safely back in his little home and workshop before the ugly night-spider people with their appalling habits and foul breath had levered their raddled bodies out of bed. The

Daimler was always tucked up snug and cosy before midday unless he was pulling an overnight visit.

A touch of a remote control snapped vanadium steel locking pins in the heavy door and he breathed a sigh of relief. Safe home again.

Home was a railway arch bricked up at one end with half partitioned off as living and work space. Not much of a view of course and it was only leasehold, but the council didn't bother him because of some obscure old railway by-law, which was handy. Keeping a low profile also helped keep the Police at bay. His greatest fear being if they found his full-of-subversive titles video collection he'd be banged up for whatever the courts decided was a 'hate crime' that month.

Carefully hanging up his other finds, he singled out the black double breasted cashmere and put it on the modified tailors dummy he used for steaming. Steam cleaning was always a good idea because these vintage clothes occasionally came with added surprise guests, like lice, and his pickier clients would never forgive him if he was to sell them gear with value added infestation.

So he had a specialised steam wand which he used to ensure the seams were visitor free. Then he'd give it a light dry and steam clean before drying on the dummy, where he'd installed a warm air blower to gently dry the fine wool without damaging the cloth.

Humming quietly to himself, he cleaned off the few bits of lint that always seemed to find their way onto black clothing, then steamed the seams carefully and went over the rest. After an hour he stepped back to examine his handiwork.

Oh yes, very nice. Just the right size for that lippy little whippersnapper who thought that because he could rap he was the bees knees. Well he'd pay for something like this. Wallace nodded quietly to himself and went to his living quarters at the back to make a few calls.

"Hey Rufus." He dialled the rappers manager. "Got some great gear for your guy. A really nice black cashmere. First quality. Should fit him like a glove."

"Cashmere? Nah. Too fuddy duddy, you got anything else?" Rufus replied.

"A red Guardsman's jacket for a little sixties vibe?" Wallace offered. Bugger. So much for that idea.

"Do me a favour. No one wants sixties stuff no more. Nuffin' else?"

"I'll keep my eye out."

"You do that son. You do that." Rufus rang off. Charmless toad. Oh well, if no one else wanted it.

Wallace went back to his clothing workshop, put on the coat and stuffed his hands in the generous slash pockets. That felt nice. Nothing quite like good cashmere. Looked good too.

He did up the three front buttons and examined himself in the five foot mirror on the wall. Very smart. Stuff the rapper, Rufus could get his own gear from now on. This was too classy to sell.

He hadn't noticed it before, but the mirror looked like it could do with re silvering, he thought, looking from left to right. He stood there for a few moments thinking his reflection looked badly double glazed.

His reverie was disturbed by his mobile ringing. "Hello." He answered. The call was from one of his occasional customers, a small time pimp called Razzle who had an 'office' two arches down. For office read 'sex club'.

"Coppers!" Razzle yelled in his ear.

"What?" Wallace said.

"Coppers! They're raiding the whole..." That was when Wallace's entry door burst in and his world became full of interest and black body armoured men carrying guns and helmets. Then a woman in uniform, or was it? It was getting so hard to tell nowadays, stepped into his workshop. She / whatever had a funny smile on her face. "Right. Turn this place over for drugs and porn. We know this little toe-rag supplies half of East London. I want it all."

"Have you got a warrant?" Wallace demanded weakly, but his heart wasn't in it. The Police ignored him and began rummaging roughly through his stock. One even pushed him aside. "Hoy! That's brutality that is!" Well, it was worth a try. Oddly enough, the officer didn't seem to see him, or even react to his presence.

"He's not here." One of the black bundled bodies, Wallace thought it was a woman, said. "Found some porn though. Whole shelves of it. Hardcore."

Wallace groaned. That was his whole movie collection. He'd given up years to build it.

"Nasty stuff." Said the body armoured officer. "John Wayne, Arnold Swarzenegger, Quentin Tarantino, John Ford. I've even found some Stallone."

"Male white supremacy filth." Said the tall woman / whatever in uniform. "Any sign of the proprietor?"

"That would be me." Wallace announced stiffly, if he was going to be nicked, at least he'd go down with some dignity. Oddly enough no one paid him any attention. "I said." He raised his voice. "That's my property! Put it back. That's private!"

"Found a blacklisted item. Stallone. Demolition Man. Worst of the worst." A male officer said, sounding rather pleased with himself. Wallace blinked hard. Bugger. He'd heard of people getting ten years in the camps for less.

He stuck his wrists out to be cuffed in a pointless gesture of defiance. Again, he was ignored. It was like being in the middle of a crowded dance floor, people brushing around and past him, but not intending to, almost as if he wasn't there.

He looked around at the searching Police, just in case he had collapsed in a corner and was having some sort of out of body experience. No. No-one seemed to be bothered either, just digging through his hard garnered belongings like he didn't matter.

One of the Police was about to use a baton on the Daimler's side window. Wallace, too far away to intervene, watched in horror, hand to mouth. Another pushed the baton wielder aside and simply opened the car door. Then the black clad figures wrenched open the bonnet and boot and started pulling at the door panels. “No-er.” Wailed Wallace,listening to the heartbreaking sounds of his pride and joy being trashed. Fabric ripped, safety glass smashed with crunching thuds.

“Anything?” Said the cruel looking uniformed woman. Wallace looked more closely. Didn't only men have Adam's apples? The black uniformed stormtroopers shook their heads. “Look harder.” She / whatever said. Wallace slumped onto a workshop stool and began to weep to the sounds of his precious Daimler being forcibly dismantled. Red-eyed he sat up and stared at the ongoing destruction, feeling a yawning pit of desolation open up beneath him. In his despair he leaned back against the big mirror and kept leaning.

Discontinuity. He fell onto his back with an 'oof' that shook him from nose to tailbone. “Oh bloody hell.” Wallace complained and unthinkingly dragged himself to his feet, taking off the coat and fussily dusting it with his hands. After a few moments he looked around in vague surprise at the echoing cavern he called home. Bloody hell. They'd stripped it bare.

Where were the Police? Where was his Daimler and all his gear? The broken safety glass? Surely they couldn't have stripped out everything without trace?

Once satisfied with the coats condition, he put it back on and made his way out of the little Judas gate in his arch-workshops main door.

Outside, the street was unnaturally busy and a street cleaner passed by in the cab of his pavement scrubber. The man waved cheerful thanks when Wallace stepped aside. People smiling? In Bermondsey? Weird.

Wallace breathed a heartfelt sigh of relief. At least he wasn't invisible any more.

Hang on. Where had all these shops and businesses come from? This wasn't his street. Yet it was, the name was the same but the sign was newer, better. The pub was open with a chalkboard menu outside. A woman wearing an above the knee skirt wandered past in high heels, talking cheerfully on her mobile phone. Short skirts? Weren't those sexist and illegal? Yet everywhere he went through familiar streets it was the same story. Although most people he saw looked well enough. He felt like he was in some crazy timewarp. Places he remembered as closed up and boarded were open and brightly lit. People seemed relaxed, focussed, unafraid.

After an hour of bemused wandering, Wallace found himself back outside his workshop, seeking the familiar. It wasn't bad here, but well, it just felt wrong.

From the other side of the road he saw a tall woman, every inch the upmarket lawyer in a well cut charcoal wool suit and knee length skirt, staring at him. Wallace reflexively looked away. Just in case. No sense in evoking an accusation of thoughtcrime. The woman, an athletic twenty something, eyes hidden by small, round lensed dark glasses, cut across the street and headed straight at him. Wallace turned around and started walking faster, trying to get away from the approaching footsteps. He glanced back over his shoulder to see she had disappeared, then put his head down, trying to look inconspicuous until a warm, very feminine voice at his elbow said. “Nice coat. Where'd you get it?”

The soft and above all feminine voice carried a soft menace, the kind you heard in pre-censorship crime movies, where the anti-heroine wore tight black leather and carried a bullwhip. Wallace froze. However, “That's not your coat.” was stated as a fact, not an enquiry or threat. “Where'd you get it?”

“Second hand store.” Mumbled Wallace.

“Seriously?” Said the owner of the voice, obviously surprised.

“Er yeah.”

“Which one?” Said the voice, loaded with disbelief.

“Oxfam shop, Perdeiu street.”

“Oh. Right.” The voice took on tones of disappointment.

"What's it to you?"

"Belonged to a friend. I thought you were him." The voice softened. "Asliana Staroth. Friends call me Azzy." The figure stuck out a well manicured hand in greeting. Wallace carefully shook her hand like it had a hair trigger although the handshake itself felt firm and sincere. "Who are you?" She asked.

"Wallace Leary. I deal in high quality gear. For the discerning client who likes discretion." No sense in not blowing your own trumpet, even if he did skirt the edge of the law now and again.

"Wallace. Pleased to meet you. You strike me as a man with a thirst. Fancy a pint? I'd like to ask you a few things if that's okay."

"Any chance of something to eat?" Wallace asked hesitantly, realising it had been at least eight hours since a meagre breakfast. At least according to his body clock. He'd settle for a Veggie but what his body really craved was real meat, but he didn't dare voice that wish. Not in these times.

"Of course." Beamed Azzy. "On me." She gestured at a pub on the street corner that Wallace only remembered as a boarded up shell.

Insidc thc pub, over a heartwarming feed of shepherds pie, made with real lamb, not ersatz veggiemeat, and a pint of well kept Fullers FSB, Wallace told his tale. Of finding the coat and the Police raid. Azzy's eyebrows climbed up her smooth forehead. "I didn't know things had got that bad. Hate speech laws and old adventure films classed as porn? Dear me. No wonder Hady turned in his coat."

"Hady?"

"Hady Israel. Otherwise known as Azrael. Angel of death and mercy." Said Azzy casually. She picked up her Martini's olive and gave it an appreciative suck. "That's whose coat you're wearing."

"What!" Wallace almost dropped his glass. He stared wildly at the sleeves.

"Keep your voice down." Said Azzy amiably. "People will think you're nuts."

After a few moments, Wallace settled. "Angel of Death? You're having me on."

"People who cross dimensions shouldn't be so sceptical." She said.

"Eh?"

"Look. You're not from this London, that's plain as day." Azzy smiled a dazzling smile. "If it wasn't for the snappy frock coat you'd look like someone from cold war eastern Europe. Worn out shirt, bad haircut, terrible teeth, dusty trousers, clean but very old shoes. Oh, and bad skin. You really need to eat healthier and wash more often. I could recommend some skin care products. If you like."

Wallace stared thoughtfully at the coat's fine cloth. Even before knowing it was a supernatural garment he'd noticed the quality. "So, apart from flip me between dimensions, what else can it do?"

"I don't suppose it will hurt to tell you even if you're a mortal. Apart from make you invisible and out of phase, yes, it can help you move between dimensions. And in time. If you knew how, but I wouldn't recommend it."

"Sorry?"

"Each dimension operates on its own set of temporal zones. Do too much shifting between them and you can end up with a really bad case of dimension lag."

"So is that what happened to Azrael?"

"Angels don't get dimension lag. We're naturally immune. Let's just say if a mortal did it too often they'd soon come apart in space and time and they wouldn't enjoy that at all." Azzy explained.

"Would it be bad?"

"Extremely."

"How bad is extremely?"

"Depends on how you feel about having your entire molecular structure ripped apart, one atom at a time."

"A human body has a lot of atoms." Wallace pointed out weakly. "Billions of them."

"True. So it might take an hour or four. Maybe ten. Very painful." Azzy grinned. This time he could see how awfully pointed her canine teeth were. "So, not a great idea."

"So I can't go home? Where am I?" Wallace said.

"To answer both your questions, no you can't and where you were. Well, sort of. It's difficult to explain." Azzy took a sip of her Martini and nodded approval. "Lovely. Always like a really dry and dirty Martini." She paused, taking in Wallace's confused expression. "I told you, dimensions."

"I don't understand"

Azzy sighed. "I suppose not. I take it you want the readers digest version?"

"What?"

"You want it simplified." She said flatly, as though to a dull pupil.

"Er, yes please." Wallace said.

"Time and space are layered. Don't ask why, they just are." She took another sip. "Sometimes the layers merge. Things and people cross between Universes. It happens. I think it might even be quantum. Angelic accessories, like that coat you'rc wearing, just make it easier."

"W-what's that got to do with Angels and Demons?" Wallace stared helplessly.

"We get to travel between all the universes. Tidy things up. Prevent the worst cock-ups. Well, we used to. Not that anyone bothers that much any more. Now we please ourselves. Within limits of course. So, you want everything to be how it was?"

"Yes. No. I don't know." Said Wallace miserably. "I wish I'd never picked this coat up."

"Really? Oh well that's hardly your fault. We'll have to find Azrael first. Only he can put things right." She idly stirred her drink with her cocktail olive.

"But he's the Angel of Death!" Wallace hissed.

"And Mercy. That's his job, yes. Doesn't make him a bad person." Azzy said defensively. "He is an angel after all. A bit morose sometimes, but he rarely sees people at their best. It's not a popular job." She leaned back against the wall, totally at ease. "If you think about it, he owes you a favour for finding that coat. Very important. I'm sure once he gets it back we can do something for you."

"Really? What we are we talking about here?"

"The angelic population. Well, half of us are actually demons, but we're all from the same mould so to speak."

"D-demons?" Wallace sat bolt upright. He farted involuntarily.

"Now, now. Keep your knickers on." Chided Azzy, giggling as Wallace's eyes widened in alarm. "If anyone was going to hurt you, do you think you'd have just had a nice supper and a pint?"

"Huh?"

"Let me explain. We immortal types have had to band together. Ever since we started getting such a bad press from the world's major religions in the early sixth century, which was when people stopped listening by the way. Don't even get me started on atheists." She rolled her eyes sarcastically behind stylish shades before glancing around. "You like it here?"

"Dunno, haven't made up my mind. The food's brilliant and it's a lot more cheerful than what I'm used to."

"Trust me, you would. Let me clue you in. This particular dimension is managed for Angels by Angels. For example, no one cares what you say, only what you do. Even then, no-one's really bothered unless people start using their fists. And we all know each other too well for that. So we can all have a nice civilised supper in the pub rather than get the flaming swords out."

"Angels like pubs?"

"Best thing you mortals ever invented. Er with one minor correction; I'm not an Angel."

"I was wondering about that. You don't look like an angel."

"Clever boy." Azzy leaned forward and patted him on the sleeve. "Was it the eyes?"

"Just a bit too intense, even behind the er..." Wallace waved his fingers to indicate her dark glasses.

"Right." Azzy said. "Technically I'm a demon."

"You don't look like a demon, your eyes aren't right." Wallace said diplomatically.

"What are demon eyes supposed to look like?" Asked Azzy with an ironic smile.

"Well, bright red, with the centre bit like a cats. Fiery. Glowing. You know."

"Glowing?" Azzy arched a well groomed eyebrow. She smirked. "That is such a cliche."

"Er yes." Said Wallace. "You're also supposed to have horns, growing out of your head sort of thing."

"Dear me." Azzy laughed in a sexy contralto. Heads turned. It was that kind of laugh.

"Do we get it wrong?"

"Obviously." Grinned Azzy and gave him a knowing look. "It's a bit of a fine distinction but all demons are female, all angels are male, well, nominally in some cases." She explained, recrossing her legs with a soft whisper of fine cloth. "We're sort of archetypes." She said with a languid half smile. Wallace swallowed, hard. Even in her severe lawyers outfit Azzy exuded so much sex appeal it was scary.

"What about God?" Wallace asked after an uneasy pause. "What sex is he?"

"No-one ever had the nerve to ask." She shrugged. "Not that anyone has asked God anything worthwhile in eons. I think even if you tried, God would be busy elsewhen. Wherever that is. Even Gabriel and the rest of the board can only get the answering service. So we more or less run our own show. Keep things ticking over."

"Oh." Wallace looked at the floor for a moment. Wheels turned. "Do you mind if I ask you something?"

"Fire away."

"Where am I, really?" Wallace finished his pint, enjoying the hoppy rounded taste.

"I told you, where you were, only not." She sipped her Martini again, then ate the olive in a manner so erotic Wallace blushed beetroot red. "The Universe is layers, dimensions, remember?"

"Okay. You said this place in managed by angels, yes?"

"That's right." Azzy leaned forward, elegant chin on slender hand. She seemed to be watching him closely, like an approving teacher with a slow pupil who is about to finally get it.

"So is this heaven?"

"Definitely not. No licensed premises in heaven."

"Well, purgatory then?"

"Nope." Azzy seemed to be taking a perverse form of delight at his confusion. "No such place. Purgatory was invented by Catholic priests to keep the plebs in line."

"You don't mean..." Wallace felt as though the floor was sinking underneath him.

"Yes."

"This is Hell?" Wallace gaped. He looked around wildly. "But isn't it filled with the worst of humanity? You know, Stalin, Hitler?" Someone across the other side of the bar chuckled knowingly.

"Not any more." Azzy touched his hand, which calmed him a little. "We disposed of them. The market in used souls is pretty moribund. Frankly you can't give them away. Even to Buddhists."

"So when bad people die they..."

"Cease to exist, yes."

"What about the good people?"

"They generally go to heaven to be virtuous all the time. Most angels find them rather tedious, which is why most of them weekend here. The rest get to choose. Or rather Azrael used to do the choosing. Now when their time comes, the majority prefer oblivion."

"So there's no fiery pits, no boiling lakes of blood?"

"Dear me no. The gas bill was killing us, financially speaking." Azzy smiled.

"So I'm stuck in hell, doomed to an eternity of having a nice afterlife?"

"Yes. Good here, innit?" Grinned Azzy. "Fancy another?"

Wallace stared at her for a moment before giving a heavy sigh and bowing to the inevitable. "If you're buying." He replied.

A Coelocanth in the bathroom

Some stories are written purely for fun, left to moulder in a half-remembered archive before coming to light and rewritten with a completely different middle and ending than the original. In such a fashion this comic fantasy was born in 2013 put into cold storage in 2014 and tinkered with on and off for five years before surfacing in the 8th Underdog anthology as a conspiracy theory satire in 2019.

Finding a four foot long fish occupying the bath was a bit of a surprise. Especially at six fifteen on a Monday morning and particularly before breakfast. "I know it's an old bathtub." Perry muttered to himself, blinking wearily at the large, strange looking fish peering dopily back at him through vaguely green tinted water. At this time of day his sleep fogged mind was still running far too slowly to register any shock. "But this is ridiculous."

Maybe if he left the bathroom and came back it would maybe disappear. Maybe he was still dreaming. He pinched himself and blinked hard, twice. No. The fish with skin like Van Gogh's starry night turned in the confined space of their claw footed cast iron antique with a sluggish sploshing and waved an amiable tail back at him.

Who had filled the bathtub anyway? Wouldn't they have heard their flats notoriously eccentric pipework in the middle of the night? And greenish water? Their venerable plumbing occasionally dispensed liquid with a brown tinge, but never green. Perry sniffed. Was that the taint of old seaweed? Sea water? This far inland?

Grabbing his electric razor, he shuffled out of the plastic tile floored bathroom with its awful bland magnolia decor, and the strange four foot long Coelacanth splashing lazily... Wait a moment. This had to be a prank, right? Sandra's younger brother was a zoology student. No doubt he found this hilarious. How the hell he'd smuggled a live living fossil into Perry and Sandra's one and a half bedroomed flat overlooking the High Street without waking them both up, plumbed new depths. Yeah, fish. Depths. Funn-ee. Not. Hang on a minute, how the hell had he known it was a Coelacanth?

Right. Close eyes, pinch self again to wake up. Turn around. He went back to the bathroom and took a picture with his smartphone, then did an image search. Oh shit. It really is..."Sands?" He called gently into the main bedroom that still looked like a bomb full of sheets and pillowcases had gone off in it. Sandra stirred, one gym toned leg visible above the sheets, the rest of her buried under the remnants of last night's frenetic bed Olympics. "Sands?" Perry called again hesitantly.

"What?" She muttered, dark bob cut hair barely visible.

"Your brother, that's what." Perry said grumpily. "He's pranking us. Again."

"If it's from the Insect house, it's your problem." Her muffled voice replied. "Oh God, it's not even half past six!" Pink rimmed opalescent eyes fluttered open.

"He's put a Coelacanth in our bath." Perry said.

"A what?" Sandra swung upright, sheets falling away to reveal her exquisite chest. Perry tried hard not to stare and failed miserably.

"A Coelacanth. A bloody great should-have-been-extinct Dino-bloody fish. I just looked it up." He passed his smartphone to her, the wikipedia page quite visible on its tiny screen.

"Don't be ridiculous!" Sandra swung out of bed and brushed past him, bathroom bound and still naked, smelling wonderfully of pheromones.

"They don't have Coelacanths at Darren's University. Or his placement." She called back. The toilet flushed, ancient sounding clangs and squeaks rattling the pipes. There was an astonished pause as she peered into the bath. "Shit!" Sandra squealed as she almost bowled him off his feet, running back into the bedroom and diving beneath the sheets. "Right!" She snapped. Perry heard her phone dialling out and walked back into the bathroom where the antique fish lazily stirred the bath water with those strange rounded fins. Behind him he could hear Sandra swearing at her younger brother over the phone. "Well, who else do I know who puts weird animals in their older sisters bathroom! You're the zoologist of the family, you tell me!" There was a pause. "Don't lie to me Darren. Get here now! Bring whoever you got to help you and get your horrible thing out of my bath!" Another pause. "I don't know."

Perry stood over the bath, muzzily looking down at the fish. The fish looked back up as amiably as its species allowed, fins sculling gently like it was maintaining position. Sandra stomped back in. "Darren says he had nothing to do with it." She said flatly.

"Yeah, right." Perry shook his head. He turned to stare back at the fish in their bath. It gazed back with oddly human eyes.

"Pez, my little brother's a world class dick, but he's crap at lying." She leaned her chin on his shoulder, and Perry took a deep breath as he felt her warmth pressing into his back.

"Sands. I've got to go to work." He groaned.

"I need a shower and there's a bloody big fish in my bathtub." Her hands crept around his waist. "I'm not going to work smelling like this. Everyone will talk, and you know what the rumour mill is like at my place."

"Look. It appeared overnight. Maybe if we go to work and come home again it will have vanished. It could even be an hallucination brought on by overwork. We've both been putting in a hell of a lot of hours recently. Maybe we're just seeing things."

"I've got a cure for that." She breathed onto his neck. Her hands crept under the waistband of his sleep shorts. "Mm. Look who's rising to the occasion." She gave that deliciously svelte chuckle he could never resist. "Time for a little neuro-pressure therapy?"

"Sands." Perry protested weakly. "It's Monday morning."

"We're both pulling a sickie." She said sharply, the palms of her hands pulled flat against his belly, her voice a sexy whisper in his ear. "I've already phoned in."

"Now you mention it, I am feeling a bit feverish." Perry shivered at her touch and tried not to grin.

"Only one place for a sick man. Bed."

"Right. Coming." Perry busily texted a sick day alert to his line manager. It saved the bother of having to do any amateur dramatics over the phone.

"Oh you will be, you will." She took his hand and towed him off to the bedroom with a giggle.

Three hours later they were lying in a tangle of sheets and pillows listening to water lapping gently in the bathtub. Perry's head was still fizzing and Sandra was snuggled up against him, a cunning little smile on her sweetly sleeping face. I must pay someone to put an extinct species in my bathtub again, he thought. Once I've got my breath back.

Sandra's phone rang. She squirmed in annoyance, one eye peeking out from under a wrinkled sheet. "It's yours." Perry told her. Her hand crept from under the covers and retrieved the buzzing annoyance.

"Darren, you little shit. What are you doing about this fish you left in our bathtub?" She demanded from under billows of cotton and viscose. Perry lay mute on his side of the bed, listening to the one sided conversation with interest.

"I don't care. It must have been you."

"Little brother, you're a terrible liar."

"Come and get it or I'll tell Mum it was you who got her car keyed last week."

"Not my problem."

"I don't care!"

"Just do it Darren. I mean now!" A moment later, her phone hurtled across the bedroom and disappeared into the open wardrobe, where it dropped into last nights hastily discarded Star Trek costumes with a muffled thump. Sandra stuck a pillow over her head as it began to ring again. And kept on ringing until the auto-answer kicked in.

"Want some tea?" Perry sat up and took the safest line he could under the circumstances.

"Mph."

"Is your brother coming to get rid of that fish?" He swung to his feet, pulling on sleep shorts.

"Mph."

"I'm making tea." He tried a more decisive tone.

"Mph."

"Was that a yes Mph, or a no Mph?"

"Mph."

"Tea it is." Perry paused for a moment, only to hear the same gentle sloshing from the bathroom. Moving into their cramped little kitchen, he filled their battered kettle and lit the gas stove, occasionally leaning back out of the doorway, ears alert, when he thought the sloshing from the bathtub stopped. Just in case that damned animal had conveniently disappeared of its own accord. The kettle whistled, Perry made two mugs of what is to many English a universal panacea, taking one in to Sandra, who was by now sitting, propped up in bed, wearing a green t-shirt and trawling the Internet for clues.

"It says here that sometimes quantum portals randomly open between dimensions and dump things into new locations." Sandra looked up hopefully from her screen. "Objects and even people slip across time and space to end up many miles and years from their home."

"Straight into our bath seems a bit, well, convenient, doesn't it?" Perry hedged, sitting on the bed. "You'd think it would more likely get dumped into some pond, a lake, another ocean, into a gutter on the high street. Even a bird bath. These things happen elsewhere, not some random bathroom in an arbitrary English market town. That's just so, you know, ordinary."

"Yes. That's why I still think it was my stupid little brother and his idiot student friends."

"You didn't give him a key to the flat, did you?" Perry asked.

"No. I'm a qualified accounts technician, not a moron. Did you lock the main door last night?"

"Of course. And I put the security lock on, the bolt, alarm and the safety chain. Before you ask, the windows are all locked, too." Perry turned and pulled a threadbare section of curtain aside, looking out of their front window into the pedestrianised High Street. Few pedestrians were in evidence on the rain swept brick paving, hurrying to get across the gap between shelter before getting soaked to the skin. A baseball cap wearing delivery driver standing inside the shelter of his van was arguing with a very damp parking attendant, waving their respectively uniformed arms at each other in a form of uptight street-semaphore. "All of them. And your brother doesn't have a key to those, either." he glanced back at Sandra. "Does he?"

"Go and check the front door." She snapped. "If he came in that way he can't have left the chain or security lock on, can he?"

"Okay." He turned to leave the bedroom.

"For goodness sake put some better clothes on first. I can almost see your bits through those shorts." She scolded.

"All right." Perry pulled on his jeans and the cleanest looking t-shirt he could find before going downstairs to examine the front door. As he thought, the safety chain was in place and the door alarm glowed a steady red, indicating that it was armed and undisturbed. He was just about to check the peephole when a loud knocking startled him. Peering through the lens he saw the fish eye distorted figure of Sandra's younger brother Darren, wearing his long dark hair in a rain slicked ponytail, leather jacket spattered with rain droplets. To Perry his sharp edged features gave Darren the air of a mildly annoyed ferret.

"Hang on a minute." Perry said loudly as he deactivated the door alarm.

"Who is it?" Called Sandra from the bedroom.

"Darren." There was a muffled thump and hurried rustling of clothing from upstairs.

"Where's this bloody fish then?" Demanded a damp Darren from the other side of the door.

"Bathroom." Perry replied loudly, fiddling with the clumsy lock. The security chain rattled off the door and Perry opened up. Darren gave Perry a sharp look as he half pushed past and jogged up the bare wooden stairs, footsteps echoing off bare peeling paintwork. Rounding the corner as Perry closed the door.

There was the sound of the bathroom door opening, an astounded pause and wordless cry of astonishment. A moment later, Darren reappeared back at the top of the stairwell, eyes wide, slack mouthed and waving hands frantically. "It-it's a Coelacanth!" He finally forced the words out of his mouth.

"Like we said." Sandra appeared behind him, now dressed in jeans and open neck shirt, dark hair neatly tied back with a scrunchie.

"W-what's it doing in your bath? I-it's an endangered species. You've got an endangered species in your bath." Darren sputtered.

"We know." Perry said tartly. He locked the door and began making his way back up the stairs.

"But, but...." Darren's voice trailed off. He waved a hand vaguely in the direction of the bathroom.

"I take it you know nothing about it-" said Sandra, icily sweet and acid, sipping tea.

"Where would we get one?" Perry asked.

"The Comoro Islands." Darren momentarily rescued a scrap of certainty from his pit of confusion. "Off the east coast of Africa."

"Well, you're the zoology student. You should know. All we know is what's on Wikipedia."

"H-how did it get into your bath?" Darren fought back a stammer.

"That's something we thought you were going to tell us." Sandra replied.

"But there's none in captivity." Darren said. "You're breaking international law!"

"Us? We didn't put it there." Said Perry mildly.

"Okay little brother, full marks for acting." Sandra sneered at Darren.

"No, I mean it. There's all sorts of rules and regulations about the transport of rare and endangered species. That's a CITES One species! On the red list of most endangered!" Darren sounded like he was really panicking. "You're not supposed to, to...."

"Not supposed to what?" Asked Sandra.

"It shouldn't be there!" Darren panic-glanced back over his shoulder.

"Well, maybe it's a Guppy that got flushed down someone's loo and mutated in the sewers, yeah?" Perry twisted the knife, thoroughly enjoying some petty vengeance for all Darren's previous pranks. Well, you could only take so much student level hilarity. Especially when Darren's antipathy toward him was so frequently obvious. Or mutual.

"Well, who do we call? Fishbusters?" Sandra said maliciously, relishing her younger brother's confusion.

"The chip shop? Tell them the special is off the menu because it's in our bath?" Perry added nastily.

"No, no. Let me think." Darren hurriedly dug around in his rain slicked black jacket and pulled out his mobile phone. "I'm going to call my professor. He might know what to do."

Perry and Sandra exchanged looks. Is he telling the truth? Perry suddenly had a falling sensation in his gut, a realisation that things were about to get even more weird. Despite that he managed "I see you find humour a difficult concept." In reply, Darren looked back at him with a panicky blankness.

A few minutes later a flustered Darren sat in Perry and Sandra's cramped kitchenette, flicking worried glances between his phone and the peeling grout above the sink piled with a weekend's worth of dirty dishes. Anything but go near the antique fish-haunted bathroom.

"Well?" Sandra demanded from the dining space doorway.

"He's in a lecture. I left a message." Darren replied.

"What did you say?"

"Just that I'd got something special. Really important."

"You didn't tell him Coelacanth?" Sandra said, one eyebrow pointedly raised. The one gesture she specifically saved for Star Trek parties, where she would play the sexy Vulcan to Perry's Captain Archer. Perry returned a weak smile.

"I don't want him to think I'm crazy. Or worse, taking the piss." Darren puffed out his cheeks, got up and stalked into the bathroom. He came back. "It's still there." He said with a harassed look on his face, plonking himself heavily into a careworn yellow kitchen chair. Perry and Sandra exchanged knowing looks over his head and left the kitchen to snuggle up on their sofa and veg out watching Netflix.

Just after noon, Darren's phone rang. Darren grabbed at it, fumbled and almost threw it in the crockery congested sink. After a few seconds he regained control of his hands and answered the call. Sandra entered the kitchenette, waiting to hear the worst.

"Hi, Professor Langmann? I've got an oddity you might want to have a look at. It's a rare tropical species that's turned up at a private home." There was a pause while Darren listened. "No, none of those. It's actually quite large." Another pause. "No, larger than that." Pause. "Well not quite as large as that, I'm sending you a picture I took earlier." A few seconds later the phone exploded, demanding specific information in tones that could be heard, even in the TV room. Then the call clicked off, leaving Darren looking pale faced and shell shocked. "He says he'll be right over. He swears a lot. Sorry in advance, Sis."

Dr Bryant Langmann PhD arrived an hour later in a bad mood, observed in astonishment and stayed in the bathroom, thin lipped mouth wide open exposing rarely brushed teeth. "Where did you bloody well steal this from?" he demanded of Perry and Sandra as they watched his incredulity from the bathroom doorway. "This is a sodding red list endangered species!" He ran a hand through badly buzz cut pale grey, almost white, hair.

"That's what I told them Professor." Darren protested. He received a sharp look for his trouble.

"We didn't steal it." Sandra said, her face saying what her mouth wasn't going to. "We were hoping you could tell us where it came from." The emphasis on "you" would have split diamond.

"If we'd stolen it, we'd hardly have made Darren call you." Perry pointed out sharply. His fingers twitched at the pompous little man who had been let in by a highly discomfited Darren. What was it with people over fifty? You'd think they owned the bloody planet. With his wide face and skinny build he reminded Perry of an ageing Otter with a beard, and just as ill natured. "You can take the bloody thing away now if you like. We don't want it." Perry said bluntly.

"I want my bath back." Sandra added sharply. "I don't care where it's going, but that fish is going. Today."

"You'll need a certificate from the Ministry of Agriculture." Professor Langmann said sharply, glancing at the creature again and stroking his face-fungus in what he obviously thought was a thoughtful manner. "That will take a week or so."

"A week!" Sandra and Perry chorused.

"In advance." Darren spoke for the first time since his course tutor had arrived.

"Why does it take a week?" Perry said plaintively. "Can't you just get some tank from the University, fill it up with water, and take the bloody thing away?"

"Interpol will have to be notified." The professor added loftily.

"Interpol!" Perry cried out. "Why do you have to call them?"

"We don't care what you do with it, we just want it out of our flat." Sandra was almost snarling.

"As it's a foreign species, the Border Agency will have to be informed. The revenue and customs too." Professor Langmann ticked the points off on overlong fingers.

"You're kidding." Perry stared open mouthed.

"And the Police of course."

"The Police? Can't we just take it to a zoo? Let them deal with it?" Sandra asked tartly.

"No, sorry."

"I'm not having the Police tramping through our stuff." Sandra said firmly. They might find her more risqué costumes, the ones she and Perry reserved for role play at home.

"I'm trying to think of a specialist veterinarian who will approve the paperwork." Langmann added. "He has to fill in the forms. Which have to be signed and countersigned by the right people before they go to the Animal and Plant health agency for approval. Possibly even DEFRA."

"That does it!" Snapped Perry, turning toward the bathroom. "I'm going to throw the bloody thing out of the window!"

"No!" Perry suddenly found himself firmly pinned in the doorway, an elbow at his throat, halitosis in his face. For a small man, the professor was surprisingly strong. "Over my dead body!" snapped Langmann, grey eyes flaring.

Surprised by this sudden show of aggression, Perry struggled to push the smaller man out of the way, but after a few seconds realised the situation was hopeless and stepped back. Langmann turned away sneeringly, took three quick strides, and slammed the bathroom door behind him. There was the sound of the lock clicking shut. A few moments later there was the muffled sound of a phone conversation. Perry kicked the wall in frustration.

"We're screwed. He's just called the Police." Said Darren. "I'm off. See you." His footsteps rapidly dopplered down the stairs, the keychain rattling loudly as the front door slammed shut behind him.

Perry looked across the hallway at Sandra, whose heart shaped face was frozen into a rictus of panic. "Shit." he said after punching a search into his smartphone. There it was on the screen. Maximum penalty two years imprisonment. "They could put us in prison. Two years. Each."

"But we haven't done anything!" Sandra wailed.

"Sands, you know that and so do I, but will the Police?"

"Erm. No." Sandra rapidly got to the answer she was dreading.

"They'll never believe us." he said. "They'll think we stole it."

"If we get arrested or even taken in for questioning we're going to lose our jobs." She stared back at him, heart in mouth. "You know what HR at my place is like."

There was a sudden heavy knocking from downstairs. “Too late.” Perry groaned.

A single slightly embarrassed looking Policewoman in high-viz yellow gave him a blank look when he answered. “Professor Langmann?” she asked.

“He's upstairs. He's locked himself in our bathroom.” said Perry tersely, working on the assumption of the least said, the better. Maybe this Police officer would simply arrest Langmann and leave them all in peace.

“My colleague will be along shortly.” she said and tramped up the stairs, leaving a trail of water as the rain dripped off her waterproof jacket.

Perry looked up the narrow stairwell. “He's in there.” he heard Sandra say tartly. Perry opened the door to another knock, and a younger male Policeman entered, giving Perry a suspicious glance. “In the bathroom, with the fish.” Perry said. The second Policeman didn't even crack a smile at the Cluedo-inspired wisecrack. He clumped up the stairs to where the Policewoman was knocking at the bathroom door. Sandra appeared at the top of the crowded landing, she and Perry sharing an exasperated look. He heard the bathroom door open and a muffled conversation punctuated by a single startled guffaw from one of the Police Officers. He overheard the crackling of radios as the Police called their base for instructions. With a sigh he closed the front door and went back upstairs.

Perry wearily trudged up the stairs, resigned to whatever nastiness the world was about to dump on him and Sandra. Professor Langmann was arguing with the Policewoman about moving the fish. “To you it's evidence, to zoology it's a precious resource.” He was waving an angry finger in their faces. Never a good idea with the Police. “It has to stay until the correct authorities have been informed.”

"What about us?" Sandra chimed in, Perry winced. Please don't Sands, things are bad enough already.

"That's for us to decide." said the Policewoman tartly.

"No it isn't!" Langmann raised his voice. "You will do as I tell you!"

The following silence could be cut with a knife as Langmann realised his error. From his position in the stairwell, Perry saw the younger officer reaching to the back of his belt. There was a glint of handcuffs.

What happened next was a bit of a blur. Sandra shouted something about it wasn't her fault that someone had dumped a stupid dinofish in her bathroom and threatened to pull the plug in the bath. She started to open the bathroom door. In response, Langmann lunged at her and the Police reacted.

A uniform cap bounced down the stairwell, stopping next to Perry's feet on the landing. For a moment he stared at the discarded headgear like it was a rain of breaded cod portions. Then looked up. Langmann was face down and red faced with exertion with the younger officer kneeling on his back. There was a ratcheting sound of handcuffs. Sandra had her hand to her mouth, the Policewoman's baton underneath her chin pinning her to the wall. There was more crackling of radios and Perry stood paralysed as two more Hi-viz jacketed officers entered and tramped up the stairs.

Hang on, something was missing. He let the police push him gently aside as a sputtering Langmann was dragged to his feet and firmly guided downstairs. The threat of violence receded. What had stopped? Oh yes, the sloshing sound from the bathroom. Sandra was being walked past him in handcuffs by the woman Police officer, tears streaking her face.

As she passed she gave him a look which said; this is all your fault. The Policewoman gave him a sidelong, quirky half smile. With a sense of vague horror he could see one officer in their bedroom examining a costume. Oh God, not that one!

From the top of the stairs he heard the voice of an older officer say. "Where's this fish then? My youngest wanted a picture to show her friends."

"What fish?" said someone else.

"Excuse me sir. Did you call us?" Another officer nudged a stricken Perry.

"No. No. Professor Langmann, the man with the beard did." Perry replied distractedly.

The fish was gone? Had he imagined the whole thing? No-one stopped him as he made his way into the bathroom. He stared. The bath was empty. No fish, no green tinted water, only the vaguest hint of sea-smell still tainting the air. Perry found himself sagging with the relief.

Another man arrived in the bathroom doorway. Mid thirties, receding hairline, wearing a navy blue rain jacket, jeans and a professionally neutral expression. Obviously a plain-clothes policeman. "Sir?" He said in a pronounced Welsh accent.

"I don't know. I really don't know." was all Perry could manage.

"You need a doctor? A counsellor maybe?"

"No, no, I'm okay."

There was a gravid pause. "Yeah, it's things like these that put a crimp in my day too."

"Does this happen often?" Perry asked.

"No." The plain clothes policeman glanced at the bathtub. A dour civilian pushed past him carrying a long lensed camera and small black carry case. "This it Dave?" The newcomer said to the plain clothes officer.

"So I'm told." Said 'Dave'.

"Another day, another non-crime scene." commented the grey haired civilian. "Could you give me some room here sir?" He said to Perry as he began photographing the bathtub and surrounding area. Perry moved over to the doorway. Dave let him pass.

Perry found Sandra in the bedroom, sourly rubbing at her wrists. "They let me go." She sniffed. He sat down on the bed and put a comforting arm around her. "They arrested that professor bloke though." She added with grim satisfaction.

After ten minutes, Dave appeared in the doorway. “Ah good. Can I have a word?” Sandra and Perry nodded mutely. “Read and sign the copies of the official secrets act I'm about to give you.” He said cheerily. “Just a formality really. Everything's back to normal, see.” He nodded back at the bathroom and handed over two formal looking documents. “Not that anyone will believe you even if you do say anything.”

“Were we hallucinating? The Coelacanth and all?” Sandra asked.

“No. These things happen now and again. What can I say?” Dave replied amiably. “It's a bit strange, but the human mind is pretty good at blanking such stuff out. Best not to worry about it. Oh, and no talking to the Fortean Times or David Icke if you don't mind. That would definitely deep six your credibility.”

“W-who are you?” Perry managed.

“Detective Sergeant Dafydd Llewellyn-Evans. Regional Anomaly Task Force.”

“Anomaly?” Chorused Perry and Sandra, who giggled hysterically.

“We investigate weird stuff like your alleged fish in the bath.” Dave explained patiently. “Not that we can do anything, just put in reports about student pranks and such.” He seemed resigned to a fate investigating non-crimes.

“You cover them up?” Perry said.

“Not as such, no. We don't need to.” Dave shrugged, handing over a pen. “Just sign where I put the X's. You could try talking to your local press, but frankly they've only one reporter left who mostly covers council meetings and society weddings. If there hasn't been a murder or a lost kitten, frankly she won't be interested.” He took back the signed documents with a tired smile. “Take my advice. Go out and see a movie. Have a nice afternoon out. Forget it even happened. I find that helps.”

With that polite rejoinder, Detective Sergeant Dafydd Llewellyn-Evans, sole member of the UK Police Anomaly

Task Force (Western Division), left the stunned couple to deal with matters in their own way. As he was closing the door at the bottom of the stairs his phone buzzed with a text message.

Oh hell! A rogue Unicorn, that rampant stallion no less, had turned up again. This time in the Tennis courts at an exclusive private girls' school. Much to the alarm of over-protective staff and thorough amusement of their upper crust pupils. Dave sighed heavily, then pulled up his rain hood and stepped out into the High Street. It was going to be one of those Mondays.

The Hunting of the Squonk

This is a completely new piece, originally inspired by a track on the 1976 Genesis Album 'A Trick of the Tail' entitled 'Squonk'. The song subject originating in a volume of surreal camp fire loggers tales "Fearsome creatures of the Lumberwoods" first published in 1910.

The well lubricated rifle bolt softly snicked a soft-nosed hunting round into the chamber. Now, where are you? Sights tracked slowly up the rough grey corrugated bark of the ancient Hemlock-Spruce.

How many days had it taken him to hike this far? Two, or was it three? It didn't matter. That damn creature had evaded his snares and traps for weeks now. He'd seen the tracks out here in the towering dark woods of British Columbia, far from any trace of humanity. Out here where the Muskeg could swallow a house and a hundred billion trees cast a dark, pine scented pall over the land. Ground that had never seen axe, chainsaw or even a single human bootprint, punctuated by massive outcrops of lichen encrusted rock, bare since glaciers last ruled this land.

Now Henry George Balmain, graduate of the University of British Columbia, Vancouver, Canada was in the deep woods seeking his Ph.D, rifle in hand.

It had started with a short contract working in the university archives after he'd made double first in his Masters degree. He was a Botanist and Geologist looking for his first real job, but the economy was flat and the Oil companies weren't hiring. So, you took work where you could.

That was when he saw a small item of Victoriana, a smoky glass photographic plate, a little water damaged but still readable with care, which had crossed his desk on the way for sorting before being sent for recycling. Administration had deemed the archive of little or no academic value, so the whole collection was being trashed. The plate's barely visible handwritten title read “A Squonk. Shot 24th July 1891 by Sir Edmund Howell-Foxley” There was also a small sheaf of paper covered in faded handwritten notes. Henry began to read. There were few legible sections on the crumbling paper, but what there was read;

Modern Observations of the Northwestern Pacific Squonk 14th November 1891 St Thomas Lake Camp, British Columbia;

Squonk is an anglicised name derived from an extinct First Nations dialect word 'Ts'a'Qu'k, which loosely translates as "Ugly little man of the trees"

Habitat and range;

Squonks are reputed to be an arboreal species, whose habitat is mainly the Western Hemlock or Hemlock-Spruce tree, native to the Pacific coast of North America (Tsuga heterophylla). Populations were reputedly once found in the range of the Eastern and Mountain Hemlock trees. Around 1880, a time of maximum habitat loss, Squonks (to use the anglicised version of the name) were once thought to have become extinct. This species was also falsely thought to have been restricted to the Hemlock groves of western Pennsylvania. Island populations were located, according to First Nations legend, all across North America and Canada.

Squonks were originally thought only to be native to the extensive pine forests of northern Pennsylvania and Appalachian mountains, but reports of similar creatures have come in from many of the heavily forested States and Dominions all across North America.

In continental North Western America, many sightings have come from the underdeveloped regions of coastal British Columbia and the forested areas of Northern Alberta. Other reports have come from Southern Alaska all the way down the Pacific coast to Howe Sound, in the south of BC. None have ever been reported on the offshore islands such as Vancouver Island or the Queen Charlotte Islands. Whilst this particular sub species of Squonk is not thought to be migratory, despite numerous failed attempts by hunters to catch individuals, reported sightings of similar individual markings would indicate that each Squonk's range may be as large as five thousand square miles.

Anatomy and physiology;

One reputed specimen, dissected by cryptonaturalist Sir Edmund Campbell-Jones (Ph.d Kings, Oxon) in 1887, who noted details of its somewhat bizarre physiology which may give a clue to this creatures alleged ability to dissolve into tears. He found that this creature has a series of large toroidal (Ring doughnut) bladders under its skin which give the animal great drought and fire resistance. Indeed, when frightened, the animal is said to void the contents of these interconnected skin bladders, possibly cutting its body weight by up to two thirds in a matter of seconds, thus vastly improving agility and speed. Squonks are clumsy on the ground, but once in the canopy can move remarkably quickly, easily able to outpace a running bear or cougar, which are, apart from man, its only known predator.

These skin bladders, when full and distended, also give Squonks an unevenly pneumatic aspect, like the deep folds of a Shar-Pei dog. These creatures are also prone to various fungal infections resulting in characteristic wart-like skin lesions. This lends an unpleasant aspect to the creature, even amongst its own kind, which has led to speculation that it may only mate on moonless nights.

A primarily nocturnal animal, the eyes are large and surrounded by light coloured fur, but lack either well developed eyelids or nicitating membrane for lubrication. However, Campbell-Jones reports large lacrymal ducts situated at the upper outer aspect of the eye, which constantly flood the corneas, keeping them moist.

Whilst few reputable images exist of Squonks, observed individuals are known to be covered with a heavily ridged mottled grey pelt ideal for camouflage whilst clinging to the trunk of its native tree habitat. Once immobile, these animals are almost impossible to spot from ground level. Adults range in size from two to three feet long from flat fronted porcine snout to stubby tail, with long spindly arms and legs which are often each long as two thirds of the animal's entire body length.

After reading, Henry searched the internet for references to these strange creatures. All he could find was a humorous treatise called 'The Fearsome Creatures of the Forest and some Beasts of Deserts and Mountains' (1910) By a William T. Cox. A similar book by Jorge Luis Borges entitled 'Book of Fictional Beings' (1969) also appeared, along with a 1976 song by supergroup Genesis from 1976, but little else. Despite this dearth of information, Henry was hooked. He slid the damaged glass plate into a spare envelope and added the notes, slipping the small package into his briefcase. No one would miss the material as it had been scheduled for waste disposal anyway. So he told himself it wasn't really stealing.

As he drove home, he reflected that despite all the camp-fire tale rhetoric, he now had exciting evidence that a whole new species existed. He drummed the steering wheel distractedly. If he went to the head of department with what he presently had, he might lose his job, such as it was. Heads of department tended to get set in their ways and more than unsympathetic to wild-eyed boat rockers. So a specimen was needed. Alive or dead, it didn't matter. Physical evidence could sway even the most intransigent academic stick in the mud.

The trouble was that expeditions cost money, which was in perilously short supply, although he did have enough money to go camping in the target area this summer. Perhaps he could borrow a quadcopter drone with a camera from the Geology department. Maybe borrow Dad's old rifle too, although the old man would be very surprised, Henry had always been so anti-gun.

Several months later Henry stepped out of a float plane onto a waterlogged jetty at the edge of a remote Canadian lake. Even under his ultra-grip soled hiking boots the rain-damp wood felt slick. With him he brought a large backpack full of lightweight clothing and a hundred rounds of ammunition, his father's old Remington 30-06 lever action rifle, a holdall containing a tent and another full of dried food and supplies and a large box containing a quadcopter drone and cameras. The pilot also left two five gallon containers of gasoline before leaving Henry standing alone.

All around the high walls of trees loomed as though they knew what they were doing. This was not some expanse of woodland encompassing a few dozen hectares, but the dark blueish green of the deep, deep pine and spruce woods. Mile after timeless mile, over hills and valleys, only permitting bedrock to poke through the gloomy pine needled canopy occasionally like small holes in a threadbare sock.

When it comes to looming, the trees of Canada's pacific north west, specifically those of British Columbia, are Olympic gold medal loomers. For the evergreen overlords of this land, looming is not so much what they do as what they are. The coniferous indigenes have had many thousands of years practice and can keep it up for centuries to come.

Two hundred metres up a gentle slope from the waterlogged jetty was a log built hunter's cabin. Nothing much, just a two room shack with log burning stove and a couple of kerosene lamps. There was a well stocked log pile, a bed and two chairs, dry kindling, a fire striker and cupboards full of canned goods, some of which, when Henry checked, were actually within their sell by dates. And after a few minutes thought he added several cans of soup and chilli to the larder. This was how the system worked up here in the back country. You always brought more than you needed and left the surplus at one of these hunter's cabins, just in case someone got stranded up here for a month or three, which was not unheard of.

While he was doing this, the float plane upon which he had arrived, a rotary engined relic from the 1960's, roared off the lakes surface leaving him quite alone. As the single engined aircraft droned off into the distance, Henry busied himself moving the gasoline and his equipment up to the cabin.

On the far shore of the lake, one of the local black bears heaved upright to stand on hind legs, sniffing the new scent before moving on. New man-thing? It moved on, that smell always brought danger. From the treetop of a forty metre tall western hemlock-spruce, large curious eyes observed the newcomer whilst the ugly little mouth underneath munched on a richly resinous pine cone. A broad, pig-like snout twitched above wart-speckled mouth and nervous finger-claws dug deeply into the bark.

Oblivious to the disturbances rippling out from his arrival, Henry continued his chores. The cabin would make a nice base while he assembled the drone and made ready for expeditions out into the greater forest. He filled the cabin's generator tank and tried the manual starter. After a few tries and skinned knuckles, the little Honda engine coughed into life and Henry had power. He laid a fire in the stove, which after a few attempts began to burn. Someone in the distant past, when they'd first built this small refuge, had drilled a well under the building, which allowed him to manually pump water without having to go outdoors. Even if the first few gallons were brown. After much pumping, the flow soon cleared and he managed to fill a large tinware pot, which he left to boil on the now-heating stove. Once boiled and cooled, he'd drop in some purification tablets. Dad had brought his youngest son up in the great outdoors and such necessary chores were hard-wired into young Henry's subconscious.

For the next few days he settled in, assembling and testing the drone, ensuring he had three sets of spare batteries, flying them cautiously up to tree top height and using the high definition camera to scan the area. He found several curious bears, who blinked lazily at the buzzing quadcopter as they raided wild bee hives for honey or munched at skunk cabbage growing around the lakes swampier edges. Just over four hundred metres away on other side of the side on the lake, a cougar languidly lodged in the fork of an ancient Maple flattened ears and bared savage teeth at the drone's buzzing annoyance.

For three more days he practised learning to fly the drone around the lakes and hills until on the third day, the drone was filming on final approach when one of the nearby treetops rustled violently, as though something had moved quickly up the trunk. Henry diverted the drone to investigate. He caught a blurry glimpse of greyish brown fur moving out of drone view around the trunk and his heart leapt. Was it? Could it really be? Or was it just a squirrel?

Pausing the drone, he zoomed back and lifted ten metres to see a series of tree tops whip back and forth as something moved very quickly from tree to tree. Henry wanted to follow, but the drone was at less than fifteen percent battery and needed to be brought in.

Quickly swapping in a new set of fully charged batteries he sent the drone back to where he'd made the first sighting. There were some small claw marks in the bark and it looked like someone had emptied a several buckets of water down the trunk but Henry was elated. A possible Squonk sighting? Checking the video, he managed to isolate a few muddy images of something that was neither bear, ape nor cougar moving quickly out of camera shot.

He enhanced the image and stared slack jawed. There it was. The resemblance to the old image was incredible. Taking an enhanced printout from a waterproof pocket he scrutinised them side by side. No question about it, the profile of the beasts head was unmistakeable, even if it did look considerably skinnier than he'd thought.

Had he really just confirmed a brand new species? A whole new genus even? Fantasies of naming this novel creature spun through his head all that evening. *Lacrimacorpus Dissolvens Balmainii* perhaps? Henry went to sleep with a smile on his face.

The following morning that smile disappeared with the arrival of four ebullient fortysomething Americans on a much larger floatplane. They brought beer, rifles, fishing gear and a collapsible boat with a loud outboard motor. Henry's heart sank. They would drive his prize even further away. He could always leave with the scant video evidence he had, but it simply wasn't enough and the Americans were too bent on having noisy fun. Of course they tried to cheer him up by regaling each other with tall campfire tales about their various other expeditions, offering him beer and steaks, but Henry, in a self-absorbed academic gloom, simply couldn't get into the spirit.

"I got a good story." On their last evening, Todd, a dentist from Nebraska looking every inch the frontiersman with his six day beard and well-used heavy wool plaid shirt. "It's about a strange creature from Pennsylvania called a

Squonk." The rest of the Americans leaned forward, taking in Todd's tall tale with amused scepticism. Henry internally braced himself, but said nothing. The Squonk was real. He had camera footage. Not very good, but good enough.

"Now the Squonk is probably the homeliest animal in the world, and knows it." Todd began. "Used to live most anywheres in the forests across the US and Canada. Geological history shows beyond dispute that, as these areas gradually changed from swampy, lake-dotted country to high forest the Squonk was forced to leave it's original watery habitat. Not being too bright neither, Squonks constantly ranged around the shrinking marshes in search of food. In the end they took to the trees." He added. "Then people came to the high forests and the Squonks, once plentiful, began their long decline. It's from these old legends that the White man first heard of this weird creature that dissolves into tears when captured."

"Dissolves into tears?" scoffed Nils, a lawyer from the same Nebraskan town as Todd. He had stayed clean shaven and his outdoor clothing was more modern. "Seriously?"

"Okay Todd. You win." laughed Zak, oldest of the four, he playfully threw a bait fish at Todd, who batted it away.

"Yeah, some guy called J P Wentling caught one back in nineteen something." Todd said mock-earnestly. "Put it into a burlap sack and all he found when he got home was tears."

"Tears? In a sack? Jeez Todd, you are so full of it." Guffawed Tony, a thin, balding man who ran a modest construction company. "Squonks, huh!"

"They exist." The words escaped Henry's mouth before he could stop them. "I've seen one."

"What?" and "No way!" chorused around the camp fire.

"Before you arrived I was test flying my camera drone and I managed to catch a snapshot." Henry produced his tablet computer and showed the few images he'd got to the Americans.

Each of them stared at the small but distinct video loop apart from Tony who commented "Kinda blurry ain't it?"

"Jeez Tony. Whaddaya want? Technicolour and surround sound?" Todd said sarcastically. He turned to Henry, whose eyes now burned with a quiet messianic zeal. "You got anything else?"

Just a water damaged picture and some old hunters notes from the eighteen nineties." Henry replied quickly. Those are why I'm here. But the drone footage I just showed you is from just last week. Squonks are real."

"I'm not convinced." Tony said after a short silence. "Good story though, even if you are Canadian. Hey, I'm turning in. You guys please yourselves. We're due to fly home in the morning and that's my floatplane out there on the water. Unless of course you guys want to go off chasing Skunks and moonbeams." He chuckled.

"Squonks." Henry corrected.

"Yeah. Whatever. We fly out at ten. Get your kit ready." Tony pushed his angular frame upright and made off toward his tent. The others followed, apart from Todd. Henry felt foolish for exposing himself to such easy ridicule.

Todd stared into the camp fire reflectively. Then he looked up at the crestfallen Henry, features sharp in the flickering orange glow. "You sure about this?" He gestured at Henry's tablet computer.

"Sure." Henry confirmed.

"So when are you going to make it public?" Todd added.

"I need more footage. Better still a live specimen."

"What do you need?"

"What does any scientific enterprise need?" Henry replied morosely.

"You talking about money?"

"Yes."

"How much?"

"For the right supplies and two graduate assistants? Half a million would do it." Henry said gloomily, expecting Todd to fall off his log laughing.

Instead Todd stared into the fire again for a few moments. Then he looked up at Henry. “What would five million get you?”

“Ultra high definition cameras, infra red, a proper technical crew plus professional guides, permits and a proper base camp with security.” Henry said after a moment, not thinking for a moment that Todd was serious. “For that money we could cover a rough circular area about a hundred and thirty kilometres across. In the deep woods, at least fifty kilometres away from any human habitation or activity.”

“What's that in miles?”

“About eighty.”

Todd gave a long low whistle. “How many Squonks in a circle that big?”

“One. Maybe. Maybe none. No one knows.”

“One? In five thousand square miles?” Todd gave Henry a sidelong look. “That's a whole lot of nothing to cover.”

“You know where I saw this one?” Henry pointed at the tablet.

“Where?”

“Up there. In that tree.” Henry pointed into the fire-shadowed gloom behind the cabin.

“Wow!” Todd said turning to look and forcing himself to whisper. “Really?”

“Read the GPS data.” Henry handed over the tablet.

There was a pause. “So it was just a hundred metres from the cabin?” Todd said quietly. “Woah.” He drew a deep breath. “You know. When I said five million dollars, that's US dollars by the way. I wasn't kidding.”

Wheels were spinning in Henry's head Over six and a half million Canadian dollars?

“Of course we'd make it all back and then some. Lecture tours, speaking engagements, presentations, books, maybe even TV or a movie deal. You'd be famous, my foundation would get a massive tax loss, amortised and repaid over five to ten years.” Todd said.

Henry was shocked. "You'd help me just to cheat on your taxes?"

What Henry had forgotten is that a fundamental difference between most Canadians and most Americans is while many Canadians have an almost pathetic faith in government, many Americans do not. Canadians therefore, when asked for extra taxes, trustingly give up their hard earned funds without thinking, whilst Americans tend to ask pointed questions which many politicians find oh so inconvenient, such as "Whatcha gonna do with it?" and will use any legal or quasi-legal means to retain what they see as rightfully theirs. Which is why the US tax code runs to over a thousand pages.

"It's not cheating!" Todd snapped and stared at him in disbelief before adding. "But if that's your attitude, I'll leave you to be sanctimonious in peace!" He firmly handed Henry's tablet back. "Goddamn Canadians!" He snarled and stomped off to his tent, leaving Henry open mouthed.

In the morning the hunter's float plane roared off the lake surface, heading southbound. None of the four Americans spoke to Henry before they left.

Feeling wretched, Henry put a pack together the following day and left most of his gear at the cabin, using it as a base camp. Every few days, sometimes a week or more, he would return to find another visitor had passed by, leaving their own contribution to the stores, but never touching his labelled equipment. As August came to a close, he used his satellite phone to access his email. There were no job offers, so he elected to try and over winter at the cabin.

North country BC is noted for brutal winters, but Henry had the foresight to cut enough firewood and thanks to several successful hunting forays, had supplies to spare. However, when he emerged, full bearded and blinking into the light of a spring morning to rapidly melting snow, he found two First Nations hunters staring at him.

"You been here all Winter?" The taller of the two gave Henry a high cheekboned look of disbelief.

"Er.." Henry's vocal chords creaked into life. "Er, yeah."

"Why?" The smaller of the two, lever action rifle cradled in his arms, gave Henry an amused look. He exchanged a rapid fire series of fluid syllables with his friend who burst out laughing.

"I'm looking for Squonk." Henry said. The laughter suddenly ceased. The shorter of the hunters scowled. The taller hunter spoke in a placatory tone to his friend but the scowl on the smaller man's rounded face did not fade.

"My friend doesn't like people bringing up old legends. He says it makes the spirits angry." The taller hunter explained. "He says it's bad medicine. Especially for white men."

"Is it? Oh I'm very sorry, I didn't know." Henry blushed furiously at the implied lapse in etiquette, which when it comes to interactions between urban Canadians and Canadian First Nations, can be quite the social minefield.

"No problem." shrugged the tall hunter. "Got any liquor?"

"Um, no. I don't drink." Henry replied.

"Okay." shrugged the tall man again. "Have a good day." He shook his head at the older man who grunted and they walked off toward the treeline in an unhurried amble. As they reached the treeline the tall man put his head back and gave a bark of laughter that could be heard all around the lake. The older man glanced back toward the cabin for a moment, then they disappeared into the trees.

Henry felt crushed. Not only had he spent an entire solitary Winter in the Canadian wilderness, the batteries he'd brought with him had died, condensation had infiltrated his tablet and caused it to fail.

Now total strangers were laughing at him. That and the generator was out of gasoline. It was time to go home, find a job and get on with the rest of his life. He was sure he'd seen something, he didn't know what, but he wasn't going to fund any further efforts with some Americans tax dodge.

Not that anyone from Canadian academe would support him. Going against established thinking was one of the many ways to academic commit career suicide. Still, he had a fund of anecdotes to help ease his way back into the social whirl, which would help him find a job. The Squonk would have to remain a mystery. He would seek his Ph.D in a less obscure field.

Later that afternoon, at a remote log built trading post and bar, the two hunters walked in and sat down at the counter with a thirtyish woman wearing too many tribal tattoos, her companion in Levi's and leather waistcoat and right at the end, a short skinny figure in massively baggy leisure pants, worn dark grey hoodie, the cowl pulled up around broad, porcine features. “Guns and knives on the bar please. Empty the chamber and keep your ammo in your pockets. Button 'em up too.” Said the gruff barman. “Then your first drink is free.” The grizzled old man put a pint glass of cold pale amber liquid in front of hunters when they complied. “Up here for the Elk?”

“Sort of.”

“Well mister sort of, I hope you got the right tags on your hunting licence. Fish and Game are pretty hot up here. Get caught with an unlicensed kill on your hood and you lose everything.”

“I know.” The tall man took his First Nations hunting ID out of his top pocket.

“Not much bear in these parts. Try another twenty kays north.” commented the barman.

“Thanks. You see that white guy at the old lake cabin? He looks like hell. Spent all winter up there.” said the tall hunter. Everyone snorted with derisive laughter. “Says he's looking for Squonk." There was an even more raucous burst of laughter from everyone but the little guy at the end of the bar, who picked up a resinous pine cone with impossibly long fingers from a basket on the three inch thick counter, putting it into his wide lipless mouth.

"That's kind of dumb." said the barman. "Everyone knows you don't get Squonk this side of the coastal range. Leastways not this time of year. Ain't that right Charlie?" He asked the little man in the hoodie.

"Yeah." chuckled the Squonk softly, picking up another pine cone to chew.

Restoration

The first half of this very English ghost story was published in the February 2007 issue of a People's Friend Fiction special under the title 'Hunter'. Beginning life as part of a writing course, I always felt that 'Hunter' was far too short and left too many narrative holes. So I wrote a second story 'Restoration' which was submitted to the same place, only to meet with a rejection slip. In 2013 I crudely stitched the two together and found that the before and after storylines actually worked. So here it is, for the first time as a complete and tweaked version of the original two tales.

"No, please, for the love of God, no!" A woman screamed before a sudden meaty crunch cut her cry short. A pause loaded with history followed, with the busy silence of a group of people guiltily dispersing. When they were gone the only sound was of rich, hot blood trickling down between massive flagstones, contaminating the earthen soul beneath.

A few cobwebs hung dustily over ornately carved oak beams, Bob noted as he walked past the medieval carvings of a heavy oak framed doorway. How did anyone clean up there?

"With difficulty." Lady Hardy's county accent followed him into the great hall.

"How did you know what I was about to say?" Bob was taken aback.

She gestured up at the offending cobwebs, well above head height. "Because it's what everyone says when they walk into the room. These old medieval places are solidly built, but they're a bloody nuisance to clean." She pointed at the approximate centre of the chapel sized hall. "Family legend says this was where it happened all those years ago."

"It's wonderfully preserved." If anywhere, it would be here. The vibe was almost tangible. He smiled softly to himself.

"Well, make yourself comfortable. Would you like a drink?"

"Tea? Oh yes; white, no sugar."

"Nothing stronger?"

"No. I'll be fine."

"Quite right. Alcohol this early dulls the senses." Then she swept out in her blue quilted stable coat, well-worn jeans and Royal Hunter Wellington boots. Everything about her, despite her relative youth, screamed 'old money'.

Bob set his equipment case down on a large oblong fringed carpet partly covering time polished flagstones. He looked up at the two metre high portrait and scratched at his cropped jaw-line beard. His hostess certainly had a number of features in common with the picture. The likeness was striking, even to the exact colour of her eyes.

Kneeling, Bob unpacked his equipment for the night's work. Digital Recorder, temperature and passive infrared sensors linked by a wireless enabled laptop computer. Oh yes, and a Stephen King paperback to while away the hours for something, or more often nothing to happen. Unravelling the charger cable he plugged it into the nearest power socket. The Cyclops eye of the indicator light glowed reassuringly. No repeat of last February's fiasco when he spent half the night sitting in candlelight with no electronics.

His hostess materialised at his elbow with a steaming mug. "If you need them the downstairs toilets are this side of the laundry. Through the side door there." Bob took the proffered mug with a poor impersonation of a smile. Mrs Hardy was paying his fee after all, and a client was a client. No matter what he thought about inherited wealth.

Pausing, Bob looked carefully at the portrait. Not a classic old master but certainly someone who had a very strong grasp of brushmanship and technique. Underneath the crazing and patina was a genuine quality work of art. "The third Countess. Staunch Catholic. Lost her head to a protestant mob from the neighbouring shire, poor woman." Had been Lady Hardy's potted history. "Ironic really, as her husband was one of Protestant King James' most loyal courtiers. When he found out about her murder, the poor man died of a broken heart. Swore he'd never rest until they were reunited. Terrible tragedy."

"So who do you think your manifestation is?" Bob asked.

"The Count waiting for his lady. That's our tradition."

"What do you think?"

"All I know is that my dogs won't come in here; and only one of the cats will."

"Oh? Cats?"

"Ah yes, Matty. I meant to tell you about our resident blue-eyed monster. He's hell on cushions but somehow the house wouldn't be the same without the fat smelly old thing. Great Aunt Gwen swears blind he's the reincarnation of someone, but then again she's always saying ludicrous things."

"Okay, I'll watch out for him." Bob abruptly turned away, leaving the mug of tea to cool. Lady Hardy ignored his veiled rudeness, putting it down to professional eccentricity. For her own part, she had a stables to run. If he wanted to be discourteous, let the nasty little man get on with his experiments. It wasn't as though he was going to be a regular dinner guest.

From underneath the worn, ancient oak dining table Matty watched her leave and lay listening to the high-pitched electrical whining with vague feline interest. After a moment or two, he stood and arched his white and black back at a familiar touch. He looked upwards to his master's chair, then at the gently smiling portrait. The master and mistress of the house were waiting patiently as they had for over four hundred years.

Above him Bob Wallis, ghost hunter by profession, college lecturer by necessity; positioned sensors, took readings then made himself comfortable, opening his book. Every so often he would peer at his laptop computer over fussy little rimless glasses, occasionally switching devices.

Around eleven that evening he looked up and listened carefully. Yes, just on the edge of hearing was a crackling, jabbering noise. Nothing coherent, but definitely there. He slipped on his headphones and turned up the volume. Classic; exactly what he had suspected. Shortly afterwards he cocked an ear to the wind complaining around the eaves, nodded with a slight air of smugness and went back to his reading. Around two in the morning, he opened his case again and took out a stethoscope. Getting to his feet he took two steps over to the walled off chimney breast, just under the ornate stone mantel and placed the stethoscope against the wall, listening with a slight smile. Matty lay under the table and blinked, purring gently. Humans never really paid attention did they? Not the live ones anyway.

Just after three he repositioned his digital camera, looking into the viewfinder with interest. “Ah.” He said as he switched to low light, exclaiming. “Oh. So that’s it.” He looked over the top of the viewfinder and a smug grin became triumphant. So that was it! Cameras couldn’t lie, at least not in infra red.

While Bob was distracted, Matty rose and in one fluid motion leapt silently onto the tabletop, where he sat purring like a minor earthquake in front of his master’s chair. Bob jerked round then stopped himself, mildly annoyed by being caught off guard.

Oh, this must be the cat he’d been warned about. Extending a cautious left hand he said “Hello you.” Matty rubbed his white furred ruff against it. With his right hand Bob turned the camera onto Matty, nodding in a self-satisfied manner. In infrared, the image was clear. All flesh and blood and most certainly a cat. Nothing untoward. So much for eccentric Great Aunts and their tall stories.

At eight the next morning he detailed his findings to Lady Hardy over a steaming mug of strong freshly brewed coffee. “Well, as far as I can tell there’s no manifestation. An iron oxide and lime reaction in the outside walls causes the chattering effect in damp weather. The clanking is a bit of old chain hanging in that blocked off chimney breast. Spirit orbs, refraction via bits of dust on sub standard lens coatings. Those ghostly forms your last investigator reported were just condensation and a draught from your cellar. As for your blue eyed cat with the unusual markings… Well, he’s just a cat.” Bob reported. “Some insulation, central heating and your ghost will disappear.”

“So no family spectres stalking the hall? Well it’s nice to know it’s not going to cause me any more sleepless nights.” Lady Hardy said with a bright brittle smile. Finding out your family phantom was a result of damp; a lime reaction and some rusty chain seemed rather disappointing. After a thoughtful pause she signed her name with a flourish before handing over his cheque. "Thank you for your efforts Mr Wallis." From her brusque tone, it was clear he was being dismissed. Bob allowed himself to be ushered out of the front door, slightly bemused by the size of his fee. He hadn't expected such generosity.

Up in the great hall Matty watched him leave; then looked upwards to the sad, patient eyes of his mistresses portrait, then across to his master's brooding presence waiting in the chair. There would be others.

Peter wheezed a little, pushing harder on the pedals as he struggled up the long straight hill. Of course he knew he carried too much weight, but that was why he'd bought this old rattletrap of an ex post office bicycle. "No gain without a little pain" as Paula, his fitness freak friend so often told him.

No matter, he had a job to do, and on a moderately sunny day like this the old rattletrap was the nicest way of getting there. His battered antique of a Citroen 2CV could stay in its rust speckled little nest behind his framing gallery and workshop today. No sense in wasting expensive petrol.

The job had come right out of the blue as these things often did. A Lady Hardy had telephoned and asked him what sort of picture restoring he did. "All sorts madam. We restore everything from frame to canvas." Had been his halfway honest response. It had always been his dream to be one of those restorers who spent years on projects like the great masters, but somehow life and a failed marriage had deposited him in a small English market town scratching a living as a small art gallery owner and part time picture framer.

"Excellent." The cut glass voice on the phone had said. "I have a painting I'd like you to have a look at."

With a slight tremor in his normally rock steady hands, he had taken down the address and telephone number. The Hardy's were well known as the last of the landed gentry in these parts. A family long-rooted in the landscape, and supposedly very wealthy indeed.

As he cycled the last fifty metres towards the big half timber and stone mansion along a long, Poplar lined drive, he had to swerve as a scruffy hatchback sped out towards the main road, a small man with a fussy academic little beard at the wheel. "Road Hog!" Peter wheezed, then stopped and took a puff on his asthma inhaler to ease his labouring throat and chest.

As he was waiting for the tightness to subside, a tall woman in her late twenties, hair pulled back in a tight neat ponytail strode across the gravel drive to greet him. She was wearing a sun faded navy blue quilted stable coat, jeans and riding boots, four Spaniels bounding enthusiastically at her heels "Are you all right?" She called out. He recognised Lady Hardy's distinctive voice immediately.

"Yes, Thank you. Just a touch of asthma."

"You must be Mister Holloway."

"Yes, of Holloway's picture restorers. About your painting." He wheezed.

"Sorry about him." She indicated the dust cloud still hanging in the air from Bob's exit. "Some people have no manners."

"Who was he?"

"Just someone else who came to see the painting I mentioned." She averred.

Without further introduction, she led Peter up the rest of the driveway to the huge medieval front door which swung open with the lightest of touches. He carefully laid his bicycle by the front entrance, furtively wishing that he'd dressed a little more smartly for the occasion.

As she showed him into a large, chapel-like space the excitable dogs stopped and would come no further, whining softly. Lady Hardy pointedly ignored them. "Here it is." She gestured at the end of the room. Hanging over a huge, ornately carved stone mantel was a picture of a slightly smiling lady elegantly dressed in the height of early 17th century English fashion.

"It certainly needs cleaning," he commented. To Peter's trained eye there were several things wrong about the picture. The subject was certainly too far to the bottom left and the two metre high canvas much too large. He ran a hand through thinning mousy hair and stepped sideways for a better look.

"Can you do it?" Lady Hardy enquired as Peter stepped forward and critically examined the frame. "To my knowledge it's never been cleaned properly in the past four hundred years. None of the staff ever dared go near it."

"Not a problem." Peter's mind was already dancing, imagining what four centuries of greasy brown patina might hide.

"Tea?" Lady Hardy saw the glint in his eyes and decided to let him get on with it, they could talk about money later.

"Oh yes please. Thank you." Peter turned and flashed a brief, distracted smile. Lady Hardy relaxed a little, at least this one had some manners.

He took out a small packet of tissues from his many pocketed photographers jacket and tentatively dabbed at the bottom right hand corner of the picture. A thick smear of greasy dust wiped off, with still more to come.

"Here you are." A few minutes later a hot steaming mug of tea was presented to him. Peter stepped back from his examination. "Who was she?"

"Ah, bit of a family legend there. The third countess, murdered by a Protestant mob just after the Gunpowder plot. Just because she was a Catholic. Ironic really, as her husband was one of Protestant King James's most loyal courtiers." She sniffed. "Poor man died of a broken heart not long afterwards, supposedly just sitting and staring at that portrait of his wife. Very sad." She gave him a sidelong glance. "The story goes that the portrait itself is haunted."

"Don't really believe in ghosts myself." Peter sipped his tea while still staring at the painting. "What does your husband think?"

He did not see the flicker of pain that crossed elegant features. "Oh, James; my late husband. He never thought much of it, but the closest you'll get to a phantom round here is Matty."

"Sorry." Peter inwardly winced at his inadvertent faux pas. He had not known she was a widow. "Who's Matty?"

"The cat? He's been with us so long he's almost an heirloom. Great Aunt Gwen swears he's the reincarnation of the countesses' chief steward." She diplomatically ignored his embarrassment. Lady Hardy indicated the portrait. "Poor man was murdered trying to defend his mistress from the mob."

"Quite a story." Peter commented a little lamely.

"Isn't it? Well, can you do it?"

"Er yes of course. There's a lot of patina, but…."

"Then I'll leave everything to you." Lady Hardy smiled brightly, turned and left, boots slapping on the stone flagged floor. As she passed through the carved oak doorway, her Spaniels got up and followed, jostling for pride of place at their mistresses heels.

So he had the job. How to start? It was all too easy to plunge in with detergents and perhaps mar an important historical document. Best to begin with something soft. This job was going to take some time and a large set of borrowed stepladders. Peter nodded softly to himself. Perhaps he should borrow a mobile scaffold for this job, maybe a van as well.

High up in the great hall, a pair of alert blue eyes watched Peter intently. Who was this? Matty slunk fluidly down the back stairs from the minstrels gallery just in time to watch the newcomer leave. Jumping up onto the big oaken table he looked desperately from the brooding presence in the master's chair to the portrait. What was this? As ever there was no answer. A smudge of paler brown in the bottom right hand corner of the huge canvas was the only indication of the strangers actions. The cat jumped lithely up onto the mantel, sniffing delicately at the oily cocktail of smells this new stranger had left hanging in the air. A painter? To profane the sacred image? His ears laid back against his head and he trembled slightly. Not with anger, but fear of failure. No, not again.

The following morning, Peter rattled up the long drive in a borrowed white box van. Lady Hardy opened the door to him and stood to one side as he carried in a huge white sheet and several cases of materials before going back out to the battered old van and returning with two supermarket bags full of soft sliced white bread. She arched an eyebrow at the bags contents but said nothing; she supposed the man knew what he was doing.

Upon entering the great hall, Peter was confronted by a white and black study in feline fury. Matty, fur standing on end, teeth bared and snarling in front of the blocked up fireplace barred his way.

He stepped back in surprise at the cat's ferocity. Dropping the supermarket bags he backed away. The cat, spitting and snarling, stalked him ferociously.

Lady Hardy broke the brief impasse by striding forward, grabbing Matty by the scruff of his neck and forcibly throwing him into an open cupboard and slamming it closed. "No more of your nonsense." She said brusquely. The howl of feline outrage was clearly audible through two inches of centuries old wood. "Sorry about that." Lady Hardy apologised. "That's the first time I've ever seen Matty rear up like that." Four deep scratch marks welled red across the back of her left hand, and several drops fell onto the stone flags in the centre of the hall. Her Spaniels whined and jostled anxiously in the main doorway, smelling a sudden change in the hall's atmosphere, but dared come no further.

"Are you all right?" Peter enquired, startled by the blood.

"Oh that's nothing to being kicked by a Foxhunter." She said dismissively. "Whatever has got into him?" She seemed more perplexed about the cats behaviour. "He doesn't like you at all."

"I've got a first aid kit in the van."

"No need. Excuse me." Lady Hardy delved into the supermarket bag Peter had dropped and took out a thick crust of bread before slapping it over the claw marks to stop the bleeding. "I think this calls for a large cup of tea." She said.

Peter was torn between his concern for his hostess and an eagerness to resume work on the portrait. He waited for a moment before tentatively making his way through to the kitchen. Lady Hardy had put the kettle to boil and was washing the blood off her hand with water from the tap over a deep white Butlers sink. "Bloody cat." She said, sniffing an involuntary tear away.

"Anything I can do?" Peter asked hesitantly, his shadow occluding the doorway.

"No, no. It's only a scratch. You carry on."

Peter retreated down the stone flagged corridor to the main hall, carefully skirting the blood spots in the middle of the hall. Laying out the sheet in front of the fireplace he brought in the borrowed scaffold from the van. Once everything was assembled he scaled the aluminium tubing to its platform and began to wipe years of grease and dust away from a three inch square in the bottom of the portrait, first with the soft doughy white bread, then with a little brush and some turpentine soap. Then back to cleaning with the bread.

After two hours careful dabbing he could make out the artists name. His heart sank a little, he had been hoping for a long lost Lely, Kneller, Soest, Huysmans or Wissing. Instead it was some unknown provincial talent. Very good work, but not the name he had been hoping for.

Working his way along the bottom edge of the portrait he noticed something unusual. A crude brown wash had been applied over the original varnish. Heart beating a little bit faster, he reached for the rarely touched solvent bottle and began to clean down to the original top layer.

A few strokes later his heart leapt with joy. A find, a real find! The bottom of a letter, picked out in gold leaf was taking shape under his cleaning brush. Peter stopped and called out

"Lady Hardy!" There was no response. He called out again, this time Lady Hardy, left hand now bound with a light dressing, arrived. "What is it?" She had caught the excited tremor in Peter's voice.

"Look, look!" Peter could barely contain himself. "Gold leaf! Lettering!"

"Good lord." Lady Hardy peered up at the recently uncovered writing. "What does it say?"

"I don't know. I think it might be Latin." Peter cleaned off some more of the brown paint. Another two letters took shape under the carefully thinned brown layer.

Locked in the cupboard, Matty felt the change and stopped scratching pointlessly at age hardened wood. His master's presence had taken on a new aspect, not the flatness of centuries old brooding but one of bright anger. Matty had spilled blood in this sacred place and now this stranger was defying his final wish! Matty slunk to the back of the ancient cupboard with a hiss and hid behind the shoe rack, trembling.

Six solid hours of work later, Peter had cleaned a strip three inches high along the entire bottom edge of the picture. Part of the inscription shone brightly in the late afternoon light slanting through high windows. He had no idea what it meant.

Two more days of gentle cleaning the brown wash were needed until he had uncovered the whole inscription which ran around the edge of the picture in two inch high letters.

As he worked, Lady Hardy would sometimes sit and watch from her place at the right hand of the master's chair sipping tea, deep in her own thoughts.

Matty, latterly released from imprisonment, would no longer enter the great hall but sat on a window ledge just inside the corridor, tail twitching, glowering imperiously down at the nervous Spaniels.

"You know, I think there's another figure in this portrait." Peter said at the end of the third day. He looked around in sudden embarrassment as no one was there to hear him. The only witness was the cat, cold blue eyes staring from the corridor.

He suddenly shivered, as though a freezing wind had brushed past his soul, but screwed up his courage and wet his cleaning brush with the dilute mix of detergent and turpentine soap he favoured.

Working with short even strokes he began to clean the coarse brown off the old layer of varnish. As the dark mess came off, new colours could be seen emerging as he thinned the obscuring top coat. Brush strokes and shapes not seen for nearly four hundred years began to come to light. With a recklessness born of enthusiasm he wetted a cloth in his bowl of cleaning mix and wiped a broad swath across the picture's surface.

Standing upon tiptoe on the scaffold platform he wiped frantically, gradually exposing the figure of a man in the robes of a Count, smiling with pride, eyes not looking out at the world but adoringly at the figure of his wife.

Carefully dabbing the last traces of the cleaning mix off the delicate surface, Peter clambered down and stood back to examine his handiwork. "Oh my goodness." He breathed. "It is truly gorgeous." He was still there twenty minutes later when Lady Hardy entered the hall and stood behind him, too awestruck to speak.

At length she broke the silence. "Oh Mister Holloway, that is wonderful."

Peter jumped, nearly falling back onto the hall's long table in surprise. "We must have an official unveiling. When will you have it ready?" She said ardently.

"Er, um, next week." Peter burbled, suddenly panic stricken at having to set his own deadline. "Perhaps three. I'll have to re-varnish."

"No, too early. Never mind, I insist you come to an official unveiling, there are people you have simply got to meet." She clapped Peter heartily on the shoulder. From the shadows in the corridor, Matty's cold blue eyes burned.

Two months later, on a warm late August evening, a taxi deposited Peter outside the Hall where Lady Hardy greeted him wearing a shimmering off the shoulder blue evening dress. With make up delicately applied she looked more like a nineteen year old rather than her real age of nearly thirty. By contrast, Peter felt awkward and overdressed in hired tuxedo and bow tie. "Mister Holloway, Peter. So good of you to come."

Peter coloured gently as she took his arm and waltzed him through the front door into the now-crowded great hall, buzzing with conversation.

Up above the great mantel his handiwork was shielded from view by a large sheet of dark green silk with the Hardy family's huge heraldic crest emblazoned upon it. A part of him felt elated that he was meeting all these possible new clients, another was nervously running through a checklist of things he should have done to make the painting look its absolute best.

Feeling a little awkward, he was gently steered to a position on the right of the shaded portrait. Here were all the people he dreamed would come to his studio to bring him work; The Lord Lieutenant, three known local multi-millionaires, several Councillors, the local Member of Parliament was in evidence with two of his entourage and a whole host of other moneyed people. Several men in ecclesiastical dress were grouped to one side of the room. Students badly disguised as waiters inexpertly weaved through the crowd keeping the drinks and canapés circulating.

Peter felt redness creeping up his neck. This was his big make or break moment. On this single social occasion rested all his ambitions of becoming a high class restorer of expensive artwork.

At length Lady Hardy clapped her hands sharply, twice. "Friends, Ladies, Gentlemen and Politicians." That last provoked a rumble of laughter from the crowd. "Thank you so much for coming. It's wonderful to see all my late husbands old friends – and a few of his political enemies." Another laugh. "For the unveiling of a restored work of art I never thought I'd see in all its glory." Murmurs of approval rippled across the hall. "My very greatest thanks are due in no small part to a man who has done a first rate job of cleaning and restoration. Without his expertise this party would not be happening." Peter coloured. Several members of the crowd applauded, turning politely approving gazes his way.

Lady Hardy raised her voice. "So without further ado, I would like Mr Peter Holloway to perform the unveiling." Out of the corner of her mouth she said; "Just pull the green cord."

A little startled, Peter reached up and pulled gently with suddenly numb fingers at a hanging green tasselled cord.

Silk slurred to the floor in a loud whisper of fine cloth. For a moment there was awestruck silence then gasps of approval causing Peter to anxiously look upwards at the restored portrait. Noises of admiration ran round the room and he found himself absently wondering if he had brought enough business cards to go round. Someone dropped their glass of champagne where it smashed on the floor. Lady Hardy stepped forward and picked up the broken glass before the catering staff could react, taking the shards towards the kitchen herself.

"That's an interesting inscription." Commented one of the men in ecclesiastical garb. "I think it reads; in the name of Christ our most holy master our love will last for eternity. Love may be delayed but not destroyed, If we have sinned in love the sin has an excuse, Love conquers everything, we are free."

Another remarked. "It's a bit of a fraud, a mish-mash of quotations from Horace, Ovid, and Propertius."

"No, no. Ex Aeternis in this context means far more. Besides, all you've done is paraphrase it" Chimed in an older voice. "You Anglicans really need to study your Latin a little more closely."

"Trust a Jesuit to know that." Peter heard the mocking aside from another churchman as the Jesuit, a lean, middle aged man in black robes, read the inscription aloud, properly intoning the syllables like a Gregorian chant.

As the tonal, almost sing-song rendition ended, Peter, standing alone to one side of the massive stone fireplace, felt suddenly light headed.

In a voice only he could hear, a woman's voice whispered. "Thank you." And there was a brief cool kiss of air upon his cheek. Then a man's voice said "Thank you." A heavy sensation of coldness wrapped itself briefly but firmly around his right hand as though it were being shaken by an ice giant.

He blinked, shaking his head as these sensations departed to be replaced by warmer, human pressure. "Excellent work Mister Holloway. I might have a similar size piece for you." It was the MP, smiling his smooth white politicians smile, pumping Peters hand with practised familiarity.

"Thank you." Peter's sensation of light headedness departed. There was the sense of an unseen door opening and closing.

"No, thank you." This voice seemed to come from around ground level as warm fur rubbed his ankles and departed. Then Lady Hardy's four Spaniels came bounding into the room, fussing and chasing after dropped crumbs and scraps. "What on earth?" Lady Hardy returned from the caterer staffed kitchen to see the dogs snuffling around, now completely unafraid of entering once forbidden territory. She was so amazed to see them inside she forgot to scold her overenthusiastic pets for begging titbits from highly amused guests.

The rest of the evening, so everyone later declared, was a huge success. Old friendships renewed, invitations shared, deals struck and oil poured on troubled waters. Everyone was unanimous on what a great social hostess Lady Hardy was, and wasn't the picture marvellous.

In the cold light of the following day, Lady Hardy sat in the great hall alone drinking a mug of tea, watching the portrait carefully. Somehow the old place seemed less gloomy this morning.

Something about the portraits light she couldn't quite put her finger on. It was quite pleasant. No longer brooding layers of threatening shadows, but a brilliant testament to unsung genius, and perhaps something more. Not to mention the memory of several quite intriguing conversations with two of the shires more eligible bachelors.

The future looked brighter today than it had done since James' passing. The house needed a new master. Maybe children. Yes, that would be nice, before she passed thirty five. This old place needed new life, a family and more beating hearts to justify its existence.

A mile away in a half forgotten corner of the local churchyard, a white cat with odd black markings sat purring on a sun warmed tombstone, almost hidden and flat among the weeds. It was a very old and weathered piece of stone, but in the right light its inscription could just about be deciphered. It read; 'Matthew Hobbs, Born in the love of Christ 12th March 1575, cruelly murdered in defencc of his mistress 19th December 1605 – God rest ye, most faithful steward'. A close observer might have been roundly astonished as bright blue eyes faded softly to a more natural feline yellow-green.

The cat purred on, enjoying the radiant warmth of the weathered stone for a while before a rustling in the undergrowth took his interest. His gaze swung round, ears erect. A mouse? Squirrel? Perhaps the Rectory gardens obnoxious little Yorkshire Terrier. *What sport.* He gracefully rolled to his feet and slunk off after the source.

Honey Tells

This is a tale in what is known as short short format (Not a repetition, 3-600 words really is called a short short) written back in 2003 for part of an evening class at South Warwickshire College.

The source material comes from real life. I was standing in a queue at Stratford upon Avon farmer's market, idly listening to the chatter around me when one of the local homeless passed by, muttering to herself. So I listened, trying to get inside the stream of consciousness ramble coming out of her mouth. This short little piece is partly her story.

Summertime, and the living was easy. Plenty of tourists, and the begging was good. Like Ibiza, where her family had lived when she was young. When Mum and Dad had been alive and times were good. Now grey old England had her back in its damp and pallid grasp. Not much sun, much less fun and people telling, telling her all the time.

She'd usually be minding her own business when the Police always came along and told her to 'move on', or those Social Workers, always telling her to 'share' herself and stop drinking so much. Why did they need to tell her all the time? It wasn't fair. When she tried to tell them things they would tell her that they didn't understand.

She'd tried to tell them she needed to use the toilet, but no-one seemed to listen so she'd had to take a dump where she was. So what if it had been in the library? When you had to go you had to go. Fact of life, that. Then the Police had come along to tell her to get out followed by the Social worker lady telling her to find a place to live.

Stuff 'em. Stuff their bloody telling too. That's what Vinny said. Go see the Sally-Ann, the Salvation Army. Sing a couple of songs for warmish bed for the night then have a drink or two to help you drop off. Probably spew up the bread and soup they gave you but that didn't matter. Never mind about little baby Carl.

Good old Vinny, always got an answer for everything. He always slept rough in the woods by the river south of town, him and his little dog Rolly. Got it all sussed with their own tent and got by, sometimes picking at the big farm where all the Russian and Polish kids worked. Couldn't understand a word they said but they were all right.

She missed her baby most. They'd said bad things about her and baby Carl. Said he'd died when really the Social had taken him away. Said she'd killed her own baby. As if! What kind of mother did they think she was? Stuck her in jail, that's what they'd done. When they released her, Mum wouldn't talk to her no more. Kicked her out. Out on the street to starve because they said it was her fault little Carlie was dead. Wasn't fair.

Then Mum had died and no one else wanted to talk to her, less it was Vinny and Rolly. They'd shown her how to get on, how to keep the cold at bay, how and where to sleep, beg, scrounge, eat and drink. How to keep safe.

Honey sat on the shopping centre bench in the late afternoon sun, watching the rest of the world scurry nervously past her and belched. Idly brushing a lock of grimy greying blonde hair from her face she tucked it under her reeking woolly hat; scratched at a stray itch on her unwashed alcohol ravaged face then took a short swig out of the plastic bottle.

She ignored the acidic aftertaste of cheap cider laced with meths. Because if she drank just enough she could still hear her dear little Carlie chuckling. Bless.

Three park benches and a bicycle rack

This tale comes from the 'stories written for my own amusement' category. A kind of Feydeau farce in which a cash strapped district council turns to the supernatural for money and finds that the rewards for sin aren't actually death, just very, very embarrassing.

No-one was quite sure whose bright idea it was, but they'd all been drinking that Friday lunchtime, so tongues and brain cells were well lubricated and running freely. The auditors had been and gone, leaving only bad news in their wake. The previous progressive council had spent all of this year's budget and a large proportion of next. When the new councillors finally obtained access to the accounts, newly elected Gerard Forthby had stared in horror, the fiscal cupboard was barer than a streaker on a hot day and they'd just made election promises they could never keep.

"We're buggered." Gerard slurred. "How are we going to set budgets if we've got no money? We'll just about cover payroll and pensions, but that's all."

"We can ask central government for more funding." said someone.

"Did that two weeks ago." Gerard stared gloomily across the pub table. "They said no."

"We could increase the Business rates." Someone else said, Gerard wasn't quite sure who.

"The High Street is half full of empty shops, as are all the pedestrian areas. No one can afford to run a retail business in town any more. There's almost no-one left to pay an increase." Gerard replied, staring into his beer and wondering if he dared have another on a Friday lunchtime.

"What about a conjuring?" Marnie Katreus, a hangover from the previous regime, head of planning and also a self avowed white witch said. "We've tried everything else. I could talk to my coven if you like." The assembled councillors gave her pitying looks. Gerard looked blearily back at Marnie's cornrow braided blonde hair, crystal encrusted copper bangles and spaced out eyes, trying not to recoil from the reek of patchouli. This was the woman who put half of the planning office out of action for days by giving out home baked 'herbal' cookies. She was also known to keep lumps of rose quartz around her work computer to 'absorb the harmful CO2 emissions' and to use words like "Operationalising" without provocation.

It wasn't that Marnie was a bad person, but she had beliefs. Everything from global warming passing through radical feminism stopping at baby seals and polar bears to Wiccan magic and beyond. Nor were her beliefs set in stone. Gerard fully expected her to come in to a meeting one day wearing a burka. Just because. You couldn't tell with Marnie.

"No Marnie, please. You can't simply magic money into council coffers. Even if you could, the auditors would have several large litters of kittens. They don't like anomalies." Even as the words came out of his mouth, Gerard realised their futility. He was right.

Just before eight on the following Monday morning he arrived to find the planning office in uproar. Desks had been shoved aside to open a large circular space in their open plan offices and some strange concentric circles filled with stars and other symbols were being carefully chalked on the cheap brown carpet tiled floor. There were a lot of antique looking candles burning and the lights were off. Marnie was in there, wearing a long loose Kaftan like robe, fussily supervising.

An earnest looking plump young woman, was that their deputy head librarian? Was on her knees, peering short sightedly through heavy black framed glasses at a large medieval book on the floor, copying certain of the symbols between the circles. Another three women in their twenties and thirties wearing long loose robes like Marnie's stood by, watching the librarian intently.

Gerard tried to push the glazed fire doors to the planning office open, but Marnie had barred them by the simple expedient of sticking a mop across the door handles.

All he could do was watch with a growing perplexed horror. "Marnie! Open this door now!" He shouted, banging on the doors with an impotent fist. Marnie looked across at him, waved absently and smiled before going back to watching her friend put the final touches to the big chalk pentagram.

"Marnie!" Gerard shouted again, mostly for effect before putting in a call to security. After navigating the call system all he got was their out of hours voice mail.

Cursing his luck, he made his way down to the security office to find it unmanned and all the monitors set to 'record'. A note on the door read "Office open between ten and four Tuesdays, Wednesdays and Thursdays. In case of emergency call our out of hours number" It cited the toll-free phone number he'd tried earlier. Bugger. He checked his watch, five minutes to eight. Fortunately the rest of the staff wouldn't be here until at least a quarter to nine.

Taking the stairs two at a time, he reached the second floor, only to be greeted by a scene out of some obscene horror fantasy. The lit candles were burning with an intense red flarelight giving the beige blandness of the planning office a ghastly appearance. Marnie and her coven were standing motionless, robes doffed, backs arched, legs wide, breasts heaving. Rigid in ecstatic spasm at each point of the pentagram, facing into the chalkmarked circle, the centre of which began to boil brilliant red.

As Gerard watched, the boiling red grew slowly from a mere handspan to a column a metre across and over two tall, with a core so bright it hurt just to look at it. Gerard, hand in front of horrified face tried to look away but could not. In the back of his mind he decided not to bother with security. This was probably something well beyond their pay grade.

The column grew in intensity, silently roiling like storm clouds, giving out sharp tiny lightning bolts which sparked between the standing coven members until they formed a net of brilliant jagged filaments. In front of Gerard the fire doors blew open and a deafening echoing voice that sounded like it ate gravel for breakfast demanded; "WHO DARES SUMMON BARBATOS, DUKE OF HELL!"

“Erm.. me? I think.” The words were out of his mouth before he had time to think. Abruptly the fiery column disappeared. The candles were back to burning normally and there were five near simultaneous thumps as Marnie and friends fell to the floor.

In the middle of the still smoking circle, a tall bearded man who reminded Gerard of a white haired Abraham Lincoln, stood looking around at the five collapsed coven members with a slight frown. He snapped his fingers, the smoke disappeared and the coven were clothed again. The man turned to face Gerard, a polite smile on his elderly face and asked. “Would you be a good sort and scrub out that line of chalk for me.” The man said, nodding at the edge of the chalked circle. “So I can finish tidying up.” He added.

A little thunderstruck, Gerard rubbed at the chalk line with the toe of his shoe, enough to reduce the line. “Thanks ever so.” The man clicked his fingers once more and the arcane circle disappeared along with the candles, the desks were suddenly back in their correct positions, coven members seated, a little glassy eyed, at various restored workstations.

“Sorry about the dramatic entrance, but it is rather expected. I'm Barbatos, duke of hell. Pleased to meet you.” the figure explained, looking very old fashioned in a Victorian high collared shirt and black frock coat. “Ah.” Gerard felt a rustling sensation inside his head. “Excuse me, just let me borrow your memory for a moment.” Barbatos said. There was another discontinuity and his clothing morphed into a modern business suit and grey silk tie, the beard now a more modern cropped jawline style. “Hmm.” The demon looked straight into the depths of Gerard's soul again, there was that sense of rustling and when he blinked, Barbatos looked forty years younger. “Much better.” said the demon. “Now, what can I do you for?” He said amiably.

“You've got a rat on your shoulder.” Was all Gerard could say.

“Oh, Crattus you mean. Say hello to the nice mortal Crattus.” The rat stood up on Barbatos left shoulder and squeaked a greeting with a polite bob of its head. “He says he's pleased to meet you.” Barbatos smiled.

“Er, right.” Gerard managed.

“Was my entrance all right? Not too melodramatic, but you mortals do tend to like drama.”

“It was...” Gerard said. “A bit over the top.”

“Was it? Oh.” Said the Demon amiably. “Oh well, I'm always open to a little modest criticism. So, what can I do for you?” The demon frowned slightly and there was that paper-flick sensation inside Gerard's head again.

“Can you stop doing that!” Gerard snapped in desperation.

“Sorry, but if all you're going to say is erm and um I've got to find out somehow.” Barbatos looked at Crattus, who gave a long and complicated series of squeaks and tooth clicks. “All right. But these mortals do get so touchy.” Said Barbatos to his rat. He turned back to Gerard. “You're a little strapped for cash I gather? Previous administration a bit profligate with the public purse?”

“Yes.” said Gerard miserably.

“So you need a little financial assistance, yes?”

“Yes.”

“Well, Hell isn't exactly a financial institution, but if you help me, I'm certain I can assist you. How does that sound?”

“Do I have to sell my soul or something?” Gerard asked pathetically.

“Good gravy no. Souls? Now there's a worthless currency. There's been a major glut on the market for centuries. You'd be lucky if yours would buy a packet of breath mints.” Barbatos replied.

“I find that rather insulting.” Gerard said stiffly, finding a courage he didn't think he had.

“And yours isn't a bad quality soul. A little tarnished around the edges but overall good quality. If there was still a market I could make you quite a handsome offer, but nowadays...” Barbatos let the sentence trail off before adding “but there is something you can do for me.”

"Does it have anything to do with human sacrifice or fiery pits?" Gerard asked cautiously.

"How dreadfully old fashioned." Laughed Barbatos. The rat Crattus was giggling too. "Nor do we take..." the demon lord stifled another snigger "Virgins." Crattus abruptly fell over and lay on it's back, quivering with laughter. "Sorry, bit of a demonic in-joke there." there was a long pause punctuated with stifled giggles. "Can we go somewhere more private to discuss this?" Barbatos said when he had recovered his composure.

Gerard checked his watch, it was ten past eight. People would be arriving within the next twenty minutes to start what is loosely known in the British public sector, as 'work'. Specifically not answering the phone, bulk deleting emails, forgetting paperwork, arranging collections for sundry birthdays, christening and wedding parties, along with discussing what was on the telly last night and what a bunch of tossers the opposition's sports team were on Sunday. Also attending meetings and holding various 'diversity' training sessions which are often deployed as a work avoidance strategy when all else has failed.

Escorting Barbatos to an empty meeting room and firmly locking the doors from the inside, Gerard sat down carefully on the opposite side of a generous sized conference table, a leftover from the previous administration, to the visiting demon lord. "Well you already know what we want. What do you want in return? I'd like to know that before we do any signing of contracts in blood." Gerard said carefully, eyeing Barbatos like one would a large hairy spider in a vivarium with a dodgy lid.

"Planning permission." said the demon lord.

"What? What kind of planning permission?" Gerard asked.

"For a retirement home."

"A retirement home?" Gerard gaped, failing to keep the incredulity out of his voice.

"For demons." Barbatos said companionably.

"Riiight." Drawled Gerard sceptically. "Do you have anywhere in mind?"

"There's a nice little spot we own in your district and would like to develop. Very rural with nice views."

"Is that it?"

"Planning is difficult. Especially for non-mortals. We'd appreciate some inside help."

"What will that get us?" Gerard asked. "In terms of money?"

"What's the price of gold nowadays? How would it be if the county archaeologist found say, ten million in Spanish gold meant to fund the Jacobite uprising in Scotland?"

"Scotland's miles away." Gerard objected.

"But the hoard isn't." Smiled the demon lord.

"You mean it's..." Gerard's voice tailed off.

"Not far away at all." Barbatos gave him a small smile. "And on council property..." The demon lord tantalised.

"You're joking!" Gerard blurted.

"On this occasion, no. So, can we have our planning permission?"

"If it were down to me, of course, but there are procedures, you know, rules." Gerard hedged.

"Which I'm assured that you will apply assiduously." Barbatos said oleaginously.

"Hang on, what about the gold being treasure trove? Antique gold coins can be quite valuable and it all has to go through the coroner's office."

"Who your council pay for." Barbatos gently pointed out.

"Are you suggesting I can blackmail a coroner?"

"No, no, no my dear fellow. Blackmail is such an ugly term. What I'm suggesting is a word here, a word there. A judicious application of some form of reward to rule in the council's favour. I happen to have heard the Coroner for Treasure who deals with your area is keen on some form of civic distinction. I'm sure a nomination for a CBE or even a knighthood from, shall we say, certain senior members of a grateful district council would not be unappreciated. Her husband by the way is a terrible social climber."

"How do you know all this?"

"I'm a demon lord of hell. It's what we do." Barbatos gently reached across the table and patted a perplexed Gerard on the sleeve.

"Do you have any plans? Ones we can approve?" Gerard asked.

"Oh yes. Arriving this morning by courier. All in perfect order. Forms properly filled in, no objections etcetera."

"No objections? Are you sure of that?"

"Trust me. I'm a demon. The Nimbies will be taken care of."

"Oh, but can I? Trust you I mean?"

"Oh yes. We know precisely where the gold is and if you agree, all shall be yours." Barbatos extended his hand. "Do we have a deal?"

"Planning for funding? This isn't a trick is it? I mean I won't have signed my soul away will I?"

"Oh for Purgatory's sake Gerard! If we really wanted your soul we wouldn't bother to ask. I mean, do you think we demons are that two dimensional?" Barbatos said scathingly. "You mortals, really." He sat back and withdrew his offered hand.

"I didn't even know demons could retire." Gerard protested.

"Look Gerard. After a few millennia torturing damned souls the shine tends to wear off somewhat. No matter how well indoctrinated you are. We're all getting rather fed up with stab, crush, scream all the time. It's become very tedious. Never mind the hearing damage from high ambient noise levels. You mortals can get really shrill. That and I know at least a thousand demons are off sick at any one time with repetitive strain injury."

"Demons get ill?"

"Sounds strange, doesn't it? Immortal creatures and all. Some of the lower ranks wanted to start a union for Hades sake. They even tried to go on strike for better working conditions. So after a couple of centuries upper management put together this plan to have a retirement home for superannuated demonic folk. Then you popped up, so we got inside that girl's head to get her and her friends to do the necessary summoning and here we are. We'll need them again to open a new occult gateway, but that won't be a problem, will it?"

"You're not going to hurt them are you?" Gerard asked guiltily.

"Certainly not." Barbatos was affronted. "We'll borrow their minds and bodies for half an hour to kick things off and then send them home with nothing more than a mild hangover and some rather fuzzy memories of a good time had by all. If the gateway fails for any reason we borrow them again. They won't know a thing. Marnie certainly won't, she spends most of her life permanently stoned."

"I had noticed." Gerard confirmed stoically.

"So, deal?" The hand was extended again. This time Gerard carefully shook it. For a demonic handshake it felt quite dry and clean, not in the least scaly or supernatural. "Excellent. I'll drop a notion with your archaeologist and away we go."

"Do I have to do anything?"

"Not yet. Just recommend your coroner for a knighthood in a week or so and we're all set."

"What now?"

"Well I'm off to file my report and we'll be in touch." Barbatos smiled. Then he was gone. Only a faint wisp of sulphur tainted the air to indicate anything untoward had passed this way. Gerard made a point of passing by the planning office, only to find it's denizens all surprisingly focussed on their jobs for once.

Precisely one week later Gerard received an excited email from the district archaeologist's office. He read it carefully with a small smile. Seven rather scruffy antique wrought iron bound wooden chests had been found in the county archives. The documentation attached indicated that they had been given to the museum by an anonymous donor way back in 1853 and sat gathering dust ever since. For the first time in centuries, the first box had been opened with an antique key found in the previous district archaeologists desk. Inside the first box was a mix of Spanish and French gold coinage and ingots. To the value of over a million pounds. The next two boxes contained mostly rough-cast Spanish ingots of about ten troy ounces each. To the tune of three million, then the other four boxes were filled with silver coin at half a million each. When he read this part of the message Gerard's heart gave out a little 'ting' of joy. Cinderella was going to the ball and they would get their extra funding. How nice of the demons to put all that gold and silver in the district archives.

A quick check on the computer indicated that the planning consent for Samiel Bros (Developments) retirement complex was progressing well. Gerard rubbed his hands gleefully. All this and gold too! They could easily afford to upgrade the old park now and might even fill most of the local potholes. On the other hand, they already had the gold, so if planning fell through...

A chittering on his desk from Crattus cut that treacherous thought down in mid stride. That bloody demonic rat had been popping up every time he so much as thought about reneging on the deal. Now it was lounging against his desk phone with an insouciance that was almost insulting. Gerard glowered at it. The rat just gave him the finger and sniggered.

Gerard affected a 'You're just a supernatural rat, what do you know?' demeanour and began looking through some of the proposals currently littering his desk. He quite liked the idea of the Gerard Forthby Leisure centre and day spa, although the cost would easily swallow up of all their new found capital.

Another week later he was basking in the glow of his own good fortune when his office phone rang. “Hello Gerard. Heard you've had a bit of a windfall.” It was Douglas Midwrent, his opposite number at the county council.

“We have, thank you.” Gerard replied guardedly. What did Midwrent want? Odious little man. “Not that it's the business of County.”

“A little bird tells me there's a recommendation in for an honour for the Coroner of Treasures.”

“So what?” Gerard feigned disinterest.

“From your office.” Drat! How had County found out about that?

“Internal post delivered it to my office by mistake.” Midwrent continued slickly, answering Gerard's unspoken question.

“Really? I must have words.” Gerard said through gritted teeth. “Not that it's anything to do with me. The lady in question is well respected and supports many good causes. We routinely send recommendations to Horse Guards for OBE's and the like. So do you. What of it?”

“Well, the timing.”

“Timing of what?”

“You finding all that lovely gold, so conveniently deposited in the district archives.” Midwrent's voice could have greased a fleet of axles. “You're not the only people to be short of funds.”

“Well thank you for calling with congratulations, but I'm rather busy right now.”

“The archives that used to be owned by County.” Midwrent continued. “At least until your incorporation in 1854. So, considering that those chests were donated in 1853, officially that gold belongs to County.”

“Really? Thank you for letting me know, but county signed a lot of things, you know, buildings, artefacts and whatnot over to the new district council at that time. Any claims on any of the artefacts within the archives would have been passed over at the same time.” Which might have been true. "Any claim from county on that basis would probably be given short shrift." Gerard said faux-confidently and rang off.

Inside his head, his inner man was running around in panicky little circles, but outwardly he was ready to bluff to the death for the money he'd braved damnation for. The rat was leaning on the phone, eyeing him meaningfully. "Go on. Report back why don't you?" Gerard snapped. The phone rang again.

"Gerard." Said an awfully familiar voice. "Crattus tells me you're having a spot of bother. I hope this doesn't impact on our little arrangement?"

"No, no." Gerard said, trying not to sound too hasty. "That is a work in progress. I'm just encountering a few minor glitches."

"Yes, Midwrent. We know."

"Did Crattus tell you?"

"No, we just possessed his PA for a minute. We've dealt with local authorities before." Barbatos said mildly. "We know what to expect. Relax Gerard. Our deal is not in danger."

"Thank goodness for that. Oh sorry, no offence."

"None taken. Crattus tells me you've been having doubts."

"A bit." Gerard saw no reward in lying. Especially when they could riffle through his thoughts at will.

"Perfectly natural. However, the money is in your hands, our planning is being expedited. Cheer up. Bye now." The line went dead. Deader than it should be, thought Gerard gloomily.

There was a knock on his office door. The door opened. It was the portly figure of Hussain Bingh, their very multicultural Mayor. Gerard gave him his best smile. "Hussain. To what do I owe the pleasure?"

Hussain sat down, tried to set his fleshy features in a smile and failed. "Hello Gerard."

"What's the problem Hussain? You look like your restaurants have all been closed by the food inspectors. Oh no, they haven't have they?" Gerard asked diplomatically.

"It's this find. The gold." Hussain said after a loaded pause.

"Isn't it good news?" Gerard asked carefully.

"Look Gerard, not to put too fine a point on it, it's Spanish. My local Imam is kicking up a stink. Says it's crusader gold and we shouldn't touch it."

"What?" Gerard said before a cynical thought bubbled up in his soul. "Oh all right. How much does he want?"

"Just a modest donation to the local Islamic centre." Hussain gave him an embarrassed smile.

"I said. How much?"

"A million?" Hussain hazarded, but his heart wasn't in it.

"He'll get fifty thousand and that's that." Gerard said firmly.

Hussain opened his mouth to bargain for more, but then saw the set look on Gerard's face. Instead he stood up, they shook hands and Hussain left. That set the tone for the next six months. Every special interest group beat a path to Gerard's office door. Each with an agenda, each effectively demanding money with political menaces. Even so, he managed to retain just over half the money for a larger project until he began to despair of ever seeing another penny. Until he came back from lunch one day to find two business suited people waiting in his office.

"Mister Forthby I presume?" The older of the two, a man with tight wavy grey hair and a slightly superior manner, greeted him with a self involved smile.

"Er yes?" Gerard eyed the pair of them cautiously as he sat down behind his desk.

"I am Milford Caine and this is my colleague Mr Compton Winyates. Treasury."

"Gentlemen. Can I help you?" Gerard said carefully, he knew a ticking bomb when he saw one.

“Your council has come into a good deal of foreign specie of late.” Stated Caine.

“Yes.” No point in lying, half the world knew. “It's got us out of a very deep hole, financially speaking.”

“Yes. We of Her Majesties Government do appreciate your recovery of such a wonderful historical artefact, however, the gold in question belonged to rebels against the crown and as such is subject to, shall we say, certain rules.”

“It's not treasure trove, the Coroner of Treasures has ruled on that.”

“And a very sage ruling it was.” Cain said with an insincere smile. “However, the gold in question formed part of a consignment meant for the destabilisation of the crown of Britain, and under the rules of conflict, like all such assets, is subject to summary confiscation.”

“What?!” Gerard exploded.

“Calm yourself Mr Forthby. We are not here to take, we are here to explain.” Said Caine.

“To facilitate.” Added Winyates, in a nasal voice reserved for only the most unpleasant public officials.

“The problem is that the gold in question originated from the Spanish Government, who have contacted the Foreign Office, who in turn asked us to investigate the matter.”

“You're not giving it back to the Spanish are you?” Gerard stared at his visitors.

“Certainly not. No indeed.” Caine smiled. “However, finds of such national significance must be safeguarded. I'm surprised you haven't had armed robbers. I take it you feel the gold is in a safe place?”

“Our local bank has a good strong room.” Gerard said nervously.

“Yes. We took the opportunity to look.” Caine said. By the looks on their faces, it was clear neither Caine and Winyates approved. “With your permission we would like to move the gold to a secure facility.” The inflection on the word 'secure' further implied that they didn't think much of the bank's vault. “Sign here.”

A document was placed in front of Gerard. He hesitated. “What am I signing?”

“Permission.” Replied Caine. “Just a formality.”

“This means you can take the gold.”

“For safe keeping” Caine said smoothly.

“Whose?”

“The nation's of course and a grateful nation will not forget those responsible for such a valuable assets recovery.” Caine's voice could have lubricated a fleet of trucks.

“How grateful?” Gerard said suspiciously.

“Shall we say four million?” Caine replied. His tone implied that this was a not to be repeated offer. Gerard sighed heavily and signed. Winyates took the document, gave a brief tight smile, then made a quick text.

“What happens now?” Gerard asked. Caine and Winyates stood to leave.

“Our security people will collect the gold and a bank transfer made to the South Carney District Council”

“Oh.”

“Good day Mr Forthby.” Caine said with a wispy smile, then he and Winyates left Gerard to calculate how much of that amount would be left. After all the promises he'd been blackmailed into.

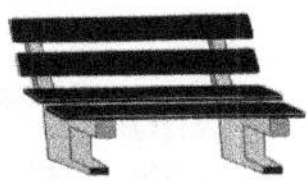

A year later, Barbatos arrived to see the unveiling of Gerard's project. “Construction of our new facility is coming on nicely.” He said. “How about yours?”

“Finished.” Gerard replied without humour. “I'm just off to witness the unveiling.”

“Mind if I come along?”

“If you want.” Gerard said tartly and picked up a large umbrella. “It's not far. We'll walk.”

“Is anything wrong?” Barbatos asked as they made their way out to one of the smaller municipal parks. The rain was falling quite heavily and gutters flowed like miniature rivers. Large puddles formed on the roads as blocked up drains began to make their presence felt. Gerard had to dodge quite quickly at least twice to avoid being deluged by passing traffic.

At the park, the project that the remainder of the gold had paid for awaited the Mayor. A very damp garden assistant stood vigil, hunched over in hooded waterproofs, obviously wishing they were elsewhere.

The mayoral Daimler arrived, the Mayor got out, cut a tape and hopped quickly back into the car before the garden assistant had even pulled off the tarpaulin. “He didn't even bother making a speech.” Gerard complained.

The big black Daimler pulled away, the garden assistant dumped the tarpaulin in a wheelbarrow and strode determinedly off in search of warmth and hot tea.

That left Gerard and Barbatos standing witness on soggy municipal turf feeling the damp soaking into their shoes. Barbatos, very diplomatically, said nothing.

“This is it.” Said Gerard angrily after a few sullen minutes. “This is all we got! After all that? Three park benches and a bicycle rack? Where did all that money go?”

“They're not even very nice park benches.” Observed Barbatos gloomily.

“And the bike rack's already got rust on it. Was it really worth it?” Gerard snarled. Following this outburst there was a long, ragged silence. Gerard Forthby and Barbatos, Duke of Hell stood under their umbrellas watching the rain falling on the council's latest showpiece project. The end bench was already graffiti gang-tagged. From behind the second bench Gerard could almost swear he heard that sneaky little demon rat sniggering.

At length Barbatos said. “The pub's open.”

“Good idea.” Replied Gerard Forthby. As if you needed a reason to drink on a day like this.

Coffee House

This is a what I like to call one of my 'coffee house' tales. Having spent more time and money than is probably good for me in various coffee shops, this is where I have made many character notes staring apparently aimlessly out of the big windows, endlessly peoplewatching.

But what if the watcher becomes the watched? And by someone who shouldn't even be there. Such thinking was the genesis of this short piece.

Colum nodded absent thanks to the Maroon shirted Barista and picked up his extra large latte; for once managing to scavenge one of the much-coveted window seats. He made a mental note of the time; six fifteen. Late enough to miss the noisy Mums and Teens; early enough for late commuter people-watching.

This was where he got most of his story ideas, staring absently out of the coffee shops large plate glass window into the street. Anything could trigger the process. A tone of voice, an overheard conversation; perhaps something slightly out of the unusual outside the Coffee Shops unfettered plate glass front window. Maybe someone interesting would drop by so he could take down some details for a character sketch. After all, what he did was all stories about people. That was what the public wanted; or at least what the editors thought that their audience wanted in his corner of the marketplace. Sad, mawkish little tales about lost love, broken relationships, hopeless romance, glamorous lifestyles and near-implausible happy endings. Who was he to buck the market? All he really did was colour in the characters a little brighter than life.

That was his big secret as a professional writer. Give the market what it thought it wanted, what sold. Never mind your artistic integrity, he'd take the money every time. Two thousand easy words a day. Most of it pulp Romance, but it paid the mortgage, and that was what counted. Melissa liked the money his scribbling brought in, and with a bit of luck could shed her teaching job next year if all went well. You could keep the Man-Booker; that never paid the rent.

Now hold on, how about a twist in the tale beginning with a reverse ending where the protagonists lose, but in losing discover true love? Worth a try. He opened his notebook and wrote neatly, bullet pointing each formulaic plot twist. Absent mindedly he noticed an elderly man in an old fashioned but well cut suit making a polite gesture towards the empty chair in the corner and waved his hand in a non-committal gesture of acquiescence at the vacant padded seat across the table.

"Excuse me." A bald, elderly and bespectacled man with a neatly trimmed walrus moustache addressed him politely. "What are you writing about?"

"Oh nothing much." Colum replied brusquely. He hated idle chit chat, except when he was researching dialogue. Besides, something about the man's middle class English accent rankled. It was precise, clipped and above all educated in a way Colum never had been.

"Used to write a little when I was your age. Sold a bit." The elderly man leaned back, looking out through the coffee shop window. To Colum's alarm he took out an old fashioned briar tobacco pipe. Noting the younger man's evident displeasure, the elderly man smiled gently. "Don't worry. I'm not going to light up. Gave all that up years ago."

Colum waited for one of the Baristas to come over and throw the elderly man out for bringing the accoutrements of smoking with him, but they didn't seem to notice the dapper figure. Ah, now that was the adjective Colum's subconscious had been looking for – Dapper. Not small, but neat and precise in his well cut tweed suit in a way that had Colum unconsciously tugging at his own rumpled leather jacket, at some subconscious level now uncomfortable with his habitual scruffiness.

"It's always interesting to meet other writers." The elderly man cocked a bushy eyebrow at Colum. Was there was a certain amused glint in those questioning light indigo eyes?

"I always find them a bit of a bore."

"Really? There is something to be said for that view. Small talents letting off esteem, eh?" The elderly man chuckled. "Of course, audiences change."

"Yes" Colum said, vaguely nettled that this anachronistically dressed man was taking up his time.

"So what do you want to write?" The elderly man smiled, emphasising 'want'.

"You mean what do I write?" Colum corrected unconsciously.

"Those trashy romances? No, I didn't mean those, but we all have to eat, don't we?" The elderly man waved away his objection.

"What makes you think that? Are you some kind of stalker?" Colum demanded.

"Heaven forfend." Chuckled the elderly man. "I'm simply taking an interest. You won a literary prize with your first novella. Quite remarkable. I enjoyed it tremendously."

"Sales figures were terrible." Colum said defensively and stopped scribbling. He'd got the message loud and clear, turning his talent to more commercial purposes after a year of fruitlessly sweating over an antique typewriter, trying to repeat his initial success. "I'd autograph a copy for you, but it's been out of print for two years. Even the remaindered bookshops don't have them."

"Like this one?" The elderly man slid a slim hardback copy across the table.

"Bloody hell." Colum recognised the first edition cover immediately.

"Steady on." Admonished the elderly man. "Language, please."

"Sorry." Colum reached for the rare volume. "May I?"

"Of course."

Colum opened the near-pristine book. He flicked to the title page, still feeling a little pride at seeing his name in print. The flyleaf was temptingly blank.

The elderly man proffered a fountain pen. Colum raised a sandy eyebrow. "Who to?"

"Just a signature." Said the elderly man.

"It almost seems a pity to spoil it with my scrawl." Colum hesitated.

"Penmanship does seem to be an unnecessary skill nowadays." The elderly man smiled in a wistful, almost nostalgic way. "What Shakespeare could have done with a typewriter. Or a word processor."

"Apart from being burned as a witch." Colum joked.

"Aha. Yes indeed." The elderly man chuckled. He glanced at an intense, bearded young man at the next table. The earbud wearing twentysomething was staring intently into a MacBook screen, an expression of confused exasperation on his face. "Social media however, might have seen him quickly dragged to the scaffold. Queen Elizabeth had quite the temper. Or so I'm told. Not a woman who brooked direct criticism."

Colum tested the fountain pen on his own notebook. It felt surprisingly smooth on the page. He practised his signature a couple of times before carefully inscribing the flyleaf, watching the ink dry for a few moments before pushing the open book back across the table with the man's pen.

"Thank you." The elderly man adjusted anachronistic round framed glasses and nodded in approval. "I shall treasure this. You should write more like it." He picked up the slim volume and blew gently on the ink to help it dry faster. When he was happy with the result, he closed the book and nodded thanks.

"I'd like to, but it doesn't pay the bills." Colum said. "Inspiration is a capricious mistress and to write really well I need that inspiration."

"Oh I don't know." Commented the elderly man, leaning back in his seat. "I've always found inspiration comes from surprising quarters. It's all just a question of letting it in."

"You write?" Colum cocked an eyebrow.

"Oh yes. I used to. Some terrible hack pieces and doggerel, but people seemed to like it." the elderly man smiled again with that wistful air. "I'd like to say thank you for this." He held up the slim volume for emphasis.

"No. My pleasure." Colum said. "Always good to mix with people of taste."

The old man stood up and began to make his way to the coffee shops door when he stopped and turned back.

"I've never been one for name dropping, but you might mention me in passing." Said the elderly man. "The name's

Kipling, Rudyard Kipling. I don't suppose you've even heard of me. Good evening."

Colum absently nodded farewell, looked down at his notes and his expression suddenly changed like the sun rising. Wait a moment. Rudyard who?

He looked up urgently, but the elderly man was already leaving the coffee shop. Frantically grabbing his possessions, he chased the figure out onto the street. Only to find that the old man had disappeared.

Bats!

This is one of the comic Dafydd Llewellyn-Evans stories, penned specially for this collection. Just a tall tale written mainly for my own amusement.

In an ancient English church, first built in the religious fervour of the fifteenth century, just before the Wars of the Roses. Something, a gravity wave or perhaps a quantum ripple, the cause is not important, triggered long dormant energies. Some change in the underlying forces of the planet tipped the scales, shifting reality just enough to lower the impossibility threshold. By how much is not important. Such things cannot be readily quantified, even with the finest instruments humanity has been able to design. There is only cause and effect.

A small shower of fine limestone dust drifted through slanting rays of late afternoon sunlight. Up in the shadowy rafters something snorted. Afterwards, silence reigned once more.

A few minutes later, a large black snowflake spiralled silently to the tiled floor where it came to rest, still gently smoking. Up in the dark reaches of ancient rafters there was a tiny soft red flare and another followed. Then another and another until the sad little ashen things almost covered the stone flagged tomb of some medieval benefactor.

That evening, as dusk dimmed the sky, the Very Reverend Penelope Denton-Clarke was on her usual evening patrol to check that the main doors were locked and that such church valuables they had left were safely stowed away. She was walking up the main aisle, directly underneath the old church tower, when her foot crunched on one of the sad little blackened shapes. "Oh." she pointed her heavy duty Maglite at the black speckled ground before bending down to look closer. "Bats?" she said after a short pause. Her voice echoing loudly in the quiet of the evening church. She picked up one of the charcoaled objects, face creasing in dismay. Turning it over in her hand as it crumbled into black dust.

"Oh dear." She looked up, shining the heavy flashlight into the shadowy darkness. Nothing.

Many people, faced with burgeoning night in a such a church, would have immediately made for the exit. Not Penelope. She considered herself a sensible person. Sensible people did not run away when faced with the unusual, they jolly well stood up and dealt with whatever the fuss was about. Not to do so would have been so, well, silly. Penelope did not do silly.

She looked down the medieval tiled Nave. Her elderly tan and white Jack Russell, Norman, was sitting in the doorway, looking upwards with a distinctly focussed expression. Normally he'd have been fussing around her ankles as she did her nightly rounds, but no, that too was odd. Nonetheless, to be worried because of what her dog was doing was not sensible either. She shone her flashlight up into the rafters again.

Something was wrong, she wasn't sure quite what, but was going to find out. No one was going to play silly buggers with her in her own church thank you so very much. She'd worked hard to get this parish and no prankster was going to chase her out of it. "Hello?" She called out. "Who is it?" No reply. She rumpled her top lip and began to walk in a sensible but determined manner toward the door. She was going to fetch a dustpan and brush from the vestry and clean up the mess before Mrs Rossersley, her volunteer cleaner, arrived in the morning. Not because it wasn't Mrs Rosserley's job, it was just that the damn woman had such a condescending way with her if there was even so much as a petal on the floor when she came to dust around the altar.

Perhaps it was time for another sermon on pride. She could write it tomorrow and deliver over the next three Sundays at the other two churches that fell to her part of the diocese. That was the nice thing about covering more than one rural parish. You could stagger your sermons. One polemic here. Another there. One sermon fits all. Yes, pride. Excellent idea.

As she was musing to herself something the size of a large pigeon flew through her peripheral vision and disappeared. She turned to follow it with her eyes, but it had already gone. She paused and harrumphed. A pigeon infestation. Well they might all be God's creatures, but they were nothing but a nuisance. She paused and stared up at the rafters, waiting for the tell-tale 'fooboodleoodle' call of one of the self satisfied little pests. Perhaps Mister Jolly from Capon farm and his air rifle would grace them with a visit?

Penelope resumed her stride. Another wafting of still air made her stop and look around. After a few more moments she felt yet another breath of air, then a sensation of heat on the top of her head and the sharp smell of burning. She reached up, horrified. Oh my God! Her hair was on fire!

Running down the aisle to the fifteenth Century baptismal font she threw off the polished lid with a clatter and drenched her scorched locks with holy water. Norman barked and whined at his mistresses plight but stayed back in the church doorway.

“Right!” Said Penelope with dishevelled determination. Well that ruled out pigeons. Some vandals with concealed mirrors and high powered laser pointers no doubt. This was a matter for the Police!

Splashing some more font water on her scorched greying bob cut, she stared down at the rippled surface of the font for a few seconds until they began to clear. There was a breath of air and she felt a small weight settle on her right shoulder, getting ready to turn around and give whoever it was jolly well what for, she glanced down at the water and her eyes went wide. She spun around, a small scream issuing from her lips, furiously brushing at her right shoulder. The weight disappeared, leaving her to frantically stare around for the source of the pressure. There was no one but her in the whole building. Breathing heavily, she stared around in horror trying to unsee what she had seen as a reflection in the unsteady mirror of the font. Wide scaly jaws. Golden glowing eyes set in an angular dark green reptilian head, grinning.

Fleeing the old church, she stumbled to her elderly Toyota and retrieved her mobile phone. Norman leapt into the back seat, cowering. Settling herself into a more sensible frame of mind she took a deep breath and dialled. “Hello. Could you put me through to the Police please?” She said shakily, keying her cars central locking as a precaution. Just in case whatever it was had followed her.

“I'd like to report a...” She began and faltered. What had she seen? Was she going to report that a miniature dragon had been sitting on her shoulder? Good grief. She'd could lose her whole living over this. She'd be laughed out of the entire diocese. Now stop there Penelope. Pull yourself together. We are far too sensible to believe in such things as dragons. Even small ones.

Taking a deep breath, she responded to the operators urgent enquiries with; “I was just assaulted. Someone set my hair on fire.... They'd been setting fire to the bats in the belfry. No, no, I don't need an ambulance.” Penelope said, briefly reflecting that the NHS did not provide emergency hairdressers. “Just a Police officer to come to St Mary's-under-close parish church. No, no, I didn't get a look at him. I was too busy putting out my hair.” She paused. “No. I do not need the fire brigade. Or an ambulance. I would like a Police officer.” Penelope gave her mobile phone number to the operator, who gave her a reference number and assured her that someone would call her back. They did not say when.

Two days later, on her way back to the vicarage, her mobile rang. She did not recognise the number. “Hello. Is that the Vicar of St Mary-under-close, Penelope Denton-Clarke?” Said a lilting Welsh male voice.

“Yes.” Penelope said carefully.

"I'm Detective Sergeant Dafydd Llewellyn-Evans, Anomaly task force. I understand you had a problem. Have you been in the church since then? Or anyone else?"

A-what-erly force? What was that? "No, only our cleaner has the other keys." Penelope put her hand to her mouth. "Oh."

"Is anything wrong?" Said the detective sergeant.

"I don't really know, I look after three parishes. Mrs Rosserley our cleaner doesn't have a mobile I'm afraid. She thinks they cause cancer. I'll have to see if anyone has heard from her." She gave him the address.

Arriving at the vicarage, Penelope was concerned to find Mrs Rosserly's cleaning bag outside her back door with a note safety-pinned to it. The church keys had been pushed through the letterbox. The note was brief and to the point. "I resign." It read. There was a sooty smudge on one corner.

Well that at least solved one problem, the insufferable woman had considered the parish church of St Mary-under-close her personal domain and had often actively discouraged other volunteers. Perhaps Penelope could now get someone she could actually negotiate with. Alison and her friends from the local Women's Institute might be a good place to start.

She sniffed at the note. What was that smell? Good grief! Burned hair? She was still staring at it when the front doorbell rang.

A dark haired man with a receding hairline over a vaguely embarrassed expression greeted her as she opened the door. Behind him on the drive was a scruffy looking dark blue Ford Focus with a single large dent in the middle of the bonnet. "I'm Detective Sergeant Dafydd Llewellyn-Evans." The man introduced himself, holding up his Police identity card briefly for her inspection. "You called the Police about getting burned in a church. There was also something about about toasted bats?" He briefly eyed the slightly crumpled note in her hand. "I can come back if you're too busy."

"Oh no. One of my volunteer cleaners has just resigned." Penelope replied.

"Ah." He said, in understanding tones. "Hard to find, good cleaners."

"Oh Mrs Rosserley wasn't a very good cleaner, frankly I'm glad to lose her. Perhaps I can get some better volunteers now."

"You mean?"

"She put other people off. Not a woman with the greatest social skills."

"Ah. Can I call her?"

"She doesn't have a phone, but I can give you her address. Please come in."

"Oh, that would be handy. Thank you." His brow furrowed. "I went to the church, but it was all locked up." He said, stepping over the threshold.

"Yes, I've just picked up the keys." She gestured for him to enter the front room and sit down on her aged sofa. He glanced around at the well-preserved furnishings as she made tea for them both.

"So." He said when she returned from the kitchen with a tray of tea and biscuits, taking out his police issue mobile. "Can you tell me who got burned?"

Penelope related her story, carefully omitting the salient detail of the glowing golden eyes set in a grinning reptilian face. Just in case. Sensible people didn't believe in all that nonsense.

After a few thumb-busy minutes he looked up and said; "Right, so you didn't get a good look at your assailant?" He asked. "Do you mind if we go and have a look?"

"Is it necessary?"

He took a deep breath before continuing. "Well, your hair's been burned and you've got hair extensions to cover the damage. Not very well done, I'd get a new hairdresser if I were you. Your church cleaner has resigned. Oh yes, and there was a slight whiff of burned hair on that ash smudged note you were holding." He looked her straight in the eyes. "So yes. I'd like to take a look. With your permission of course. Or do I need a warrant?"

Penelope bridled at the criticism, but bit down on her embarrassed anger. The jibe about a better hairdresser had been particularly annoying. "Very well, but I don't know what you expect to see."

At the church they were greeted by a puzzled middle aged woman sitting in a Florist's van. "I was supposed to meet a Mrs Rosserley to confirm the flower arrangement for the Fisher wedding on Friday." She said. "When I went to her address she just swore at me through the letterbox and told me to go away."

"Oh dear." Said Penelope. "I've never heard her swear. Whatever happened must be bad."

"Okay." Said Dave decisively. "I'd better go first. See what's what."

"Shouldn't you get reinforcements? A SWAT team or something?"

"This is South Cheshire, not the United States." Dave chuckled and held his right hand out for the keys. Penelope handed the jangling bunch over. After a minute fiddling with the outsize antiques he managed to unlock the main door. "Right." He said grittily, opening the Judas gate in the massive oak portal and slipping inside, closing it with a hefty clunk.

"Is he doing something dangerous?" Said the Florist in tones of mild concern.

"I don't know." Said Penelope. "He might be."

"Is it wild animals? A badger or something?" The Florist asked.

"Not a clue. We'll know in a minute." Penelope lied. She chatted with the Florist to pass the time, angling for inside information on her hopefully happily married couple to be.

Just inside the echoing silence of the old church, Dave stopped and stood by the main door, looking around carefully, noting the bizarre limestone carvings in the shadows, a grotesque face here, a dragon-like gargoyle there. All very medieval.

In the middle of the aisle between heavy wooden pews was an incongruously bright yellow bucket lying on its side and a large dried up water stain on the old tile floor. The remnants of dried soap suds still showing the outer limit of the spillage. So, this was where the cleaner had been when she was attacked. Moving slowly, Dave took a flashlight out of his coat pocket and walked quietly around the side of the church, keeping fairly close to the wall, looking up at tall and narrow stained glass windows which had somehow escaped the iconoclastic predations of both Henry VIII and the English civil war. Just past the altar, the ornate tomb of a medieval knight or some other armoured local notable stared eternally up at the rafters. He wondered idly why such people were always portrayed in chain mail and armour. Was his anticipated afterlife that hazardous?

Dave ducked involuntarily as something fluttered past. A small waft of methane and billow of warm air passed over the top of his head with a soft 'whomp' as he did so.

What the hell was that? He twisted around sharply to see something, he wasn't quite sure what, flutter off into the shadows.

“Bloody hell.” He swore reflexively. “Someone's armed the pigeons.” Although if he thought about it, that hadn't sounded like the distinctive slapping of pigeons wings.

Oh. He looked down. A charred pigeon, half eaten, lay at his feet. Taking a picture with his phone he checked the signal. No bars. Bugger.

Moving quickly, he walked up the side aisle to just level with the altar. A small sound made him turn around to see something bright green and scaly diving straight at him. He dodged, letting whatever it was swoop past with a flutter of leathery wings to swing back up into the shadows. “Dragons?” He said in astonishment. Pointing his flashlight up into the rafter shadowed darkness he saw the reflections of twin golden lights. Tiny dragons? Well it would certainly account for the charred bat and pigeon bodies.

Swiftly striding down the side aisle, he skipped over the dead pigeon and ducked another swooping attack. Right. This looked could be a job for Ozzie.

No point calling this one in to base, no one would ever believe him, but that was probably why he'd been given the job in the first place. He was 'Sensible Dave', who never bothered the higher ups with complications if he could help it. If the Americans had task forces for everything under the sun, the Justice department had told him, then so could the British Police Service. Pity they didn't have the budget for more than one Detective Sergeant for half the ruddy country of course. The Twitter Squad, chasing silly buggers who were rude to people online, had at least twenty dedicated constables and other ranks per county. Per county! And none of the lazy sods worked weekends. Taking a deep breath, he launched himself toward the exit and sprinted the last five metres to the main door, twisting through and slamming the door behind him. From the other side of the door there was a soft 'phut' and the smell of burning marsh gas. Right, That did it.

The vicar and florist stood looking at him as though he'd just stepped off a UFO. Pausing until his heart had slowed to something approximating normal, he nodded politely at them and carefully locked the church door. "Well." He said, trying to keep the mad cheerfulness out of his voice. "I think I know what the problem is."

Pulling out his mobile, he made a call. "Hello, is that Ozzie. It's Dave. Have you got anything urgent going on? Oh good. I've got a a job for you. A special. At a church called St Mary's-under-close. I'll text you the details. Oh, there's handy for you." He looked up at Penelope and the Florist. "Ozzie is a specialist pest control officer. He says he can be here by four and done by seven. How does that sound?"

"When can we get into the church?" Penelope asked.

"Not until pest control have done their job. He's usually very good."

"Oh. Very nice. I suppose." Penelope paused uncertainly. "Does he kill whatever it is?"

"I don't know. You'd have to ask him."

"Well if he intends to kill the poor creatures, he's not to come." She said decisively.

"Pardon?" Dave looked at her incredulously. "Well, I'll give Ozzie another call and see what he wants to do with your infestation." He redialled. "Hi Ozzie, it's Dave again. Vicar says you're not to kill whatever our infestation is." He listened for a moment. "Dunno." Another pause. "Oh, that's all right then." Dave turned to Penelope. "He says they don't usually. Unless its rats or mice he mainly does catch and release. Too many endangered species, so he says."

"Well, what do they do with them?" Penelope was still indignant.

"I don't know. Pest Services are generally very humane."

"They don't just take them away and gas them or something?" She insisted.

Dave spoke into his mobile. "Did you hear that Oz?" There was an affirmative noise from the other end of the line. "Ozzie says they don't kill special creatures."

"Special? Can he guarantee that?"

"You heard that Oz? Oh, right." There were more noises from Dave's mobile. He looked at Penelope again. "He says he'll be over in a couple of hours. I'll wait here."

"Are you all right officer?" Penelope enquired.

"Who me? All part of the job." Dave said with a brightness he didn't feel and watched the vicar leave in the Florists van.

An hour later as he was scrunched up in his dark blue Ford Focus writing up a report, a nondescript grey van crunched up into the Church's gravel car park. A short, barrel shaped dark skinned man with a shaven head swung out of the cab after it rolled to a halt. The short man recognised Dave and waved a cheerful greeting. Dave got out of his car.

"Allo Dave, cher ami." 'Ozzie' said in a heavy French accent. "You 'as ze tiny dragoons?"

"Hello Ozzie. That's right. Frisky little beggars. Singed the vicars hair, terrorised a cleaner and had a go at scorching me."

"Yeah, yeah. We go see your tiny dragoons, oui?" Ozzie grinned back. Dave handed him the keys. Ozzie opened the church door briefly and sniffed. "Not dragoons." He shook his head. "Wyverns." He pronounced it in the French fashion 'why-verns'

"What?" Dave looked at him incredulously.

"Ver, ver nasty. No dragoons. Two legs no' four. Gold eyes. Burp methane. Eat bats and pigeons." Ozzie explained with a gallic shrug. "You watch ze big tail, got a stinger."

"What? Like poisonous." Dave immediately regretted his bravado at having gone into the church alone.

"Non. C'est – eet like a wasp. Hurts. Alkaloid. Put vinegar on – no pain." He grinned at Dave's alarmed expression.

"Hang on. Wyverns you say?" Dave checked his smartphone. "But they're mythical."

Ozzie laughed. "So something mythical eet chase you."

"All right. So what are you going to do about it?" Dave asked. Ozzie smiled and retrieved two heavy black golf umbrellas from the back of his van.

"We go take a look." Ozzie's grin widened.

The small man sauntered off to the church and slid sideways through the door. Dave hurried after him and found Ozzie, umbrella deployed, just inside the old building, looking around intently. Something fluttered overhead but this time there was no smell of methane. Ozzie signalled at him to open his black golf umbrella.

“I thought it was unlucky to open an umbrella indoors.” He said to Ozzie in a stage whisper.

“Not eef you don' want to get tres croustillant.” Ozzie favoured him with a sidelong look he reserved for idiots.

“All right, all right, but if anything happens, I told you so.” Dave replied testily.

“See?” Ozzie pointed at the top of an arch column.

“What?”

“Where ze Wyvern, she come from.”

“I don't see anything.”

“Zat ees because it is no longer zere.” Ozzie replied with an air of disdain. “ze Wyvern was zere.”

“Don't be daft. That's just where the builders left out a carving.”

Ozzie rolled his eyes and pointed forcibly. “Non. Ze Wyvern was carved in ze stone.”

“So you're saying it just came to life? Go on.”

“Ze Wyvern was a statue.” Said Ozzie in tones designed to convey disdain. “Now eet ees not.”

“Can't we just leave the door open and let it fly away?”

Ozzie gave him a look so old fashioned it could be used to value antiques. “Non.” He said flatly.

“So what are you going to do?”

“Reset ze building's karmic signature.” Ozzie repeated. “C'est tres difficile. But fortunately.” He paused for effect. “I am only registered witch doctor for ze western of UK.”

“Oh.” Said Dave. “Didn't know witch doctors had to be registered.”

“Also licensed Voodoo doctor, Wangateur, Acupuncturist and qualified Druid.” Ozzie said loftily.

“So what are you doing in pest control?”

“Ees a hobby.” Ozzie shrugged and led the way outside. As they closed the door behind them there was another belch of burning methane.

“You know Ozzie. I could get really tired of Wyverns.”

“Hokay.” Ozzie beckoned him over to his van. “I mix ze potion. You put one of zese at each corner.” He handed over a sack containing dozens of bones. “Do not lose.” Ozzie admonished sternly.

Dave walked around the old church, wedging a bone carefully at each corner. After he was finished he reached into the sack one more time and felt a horribly familiar shape. Pulling out a human skull he stared in at it horror. “Ozzie!” Dave could feel his bowels beginning to liquefy.

“What ees eet?” Ozzie walked around the corner carrying a large clay pot. “Hey! Put zat back!” He said sharply.

“Who is this?” Dave asked suspiciously, having gotten over his initial fright.

“Mon Grandmere, grandmother. Ver' great Hougan. High Queen of Voodoo eight years running in occult Olympics. Show respec monsieur Dave.”

“Why are you carrying her skull around then? How did she die?” Dave asked suspiciously.

“Not really dead. She just not ready to retire.” Ozzie shrugged.

“And you can take zose grubby feengers from my eye sockets.” Said a thin, whispery voice from Dave's right hand. He almost dropped the skull in fright.

“Oh. Sorry.” With trembling fingers, Dave gently placed the undead skull back in the bag.

Ozzie led him back to the church front door, placed the pot on the floor and lit a cigarette. “Don't you have to wear a special outfit?” Asked Dave, still a little shell shocked.

“Non.” Ozzie took a deep drag of strong tobacco and blew smoke out of his nose at the door. “I did but eet chafe too much. Grass gussets.” He explained.

Dave handed the sack containing Ozzie's grandmother back carefully. As he watched, the cigarette smoke thickened and flowed around centuries old stone, sinuously wrapping itself about the venerable old building like sentient fog. Then Ozzie threw his half smoked cigarette in the pot, there was a whoosh! a bright flare of light and the smoke cloud disappeared.

Ozzie looked at his handiwork with a nod of satisfaction and opened the church door before stepping inside. Dave followed. The Wyvern was sitting back on top of the once empty column, a mythical medieval study in stone. Ozzie took his cell phone out of his pocket, made a few calculations and handed it over to Dave. “Ze bill.” He said.

Dave raised eyebrows at the amount. “Two thousand three hundred and fifty one and thirty pee? Isn't that a bit expensive?”

“Blame ze VAT.” Said Ozzie darkly. “You get accounts to claim eet back.” Once Dave had signed the phone app he took it back, picked up his grandmothers bones and carefully collected those Dave had placed around the church.

As he watched the little Cameroonian drive away, Dave idly wondered how he'd fill in the incident report for this one. Oh well, at least home was only an hours drive away, traffic permitting.

Th-th-that's all folks

www.ingramcontent.com/pod-product-compliance
Lightning Source LLC
Chambersburg PA
CBHW070628310726
48982CB00001B/203

* 9 7 8 1 7 7 7 0 4 0 1 0 9 *